WEE ROW OF SHOPS AND A BAR

Plus other short stories

Mary Lewsley

Grosvenor House
Publishing Limited

All rights reserved
Copyright © Mary Lewsley, 2022

The right of Mary Lewsley to be identified as the author of this
work has been asserted in accordance with Section 78
of the Copyright, Designs and Patents Act 1988

The book cover is copyright to Mary Lewsley

This book is published by
Grosvenor House Publishing Ltd
Link House
140 The Broadway, Tolworth, Surrey, KT6 7HT.
www.grosvenorhousepublishing.co.uk

This book is sold subject to the conditions that it shall not, by way of
trade or otherwise, be lent, resold, hired out or otherwise circulated
without the author's or publisher's prior consent in any form of binding or
cover other than that in which it is published and
without a similar condition including this condition being imposed
on the subsequent purchaser.

This book is a work of fiction. Any resemblance to
people or events, past or present, is purely coincidental.

A CIP record for this book
is available from the British Library

ISBN 978-1-83975-910-9

About the Author

Mary Lewsley is the pen name of Maureen McMullan.

She was born in Birmingham to Irish parents.

Mary Lewsley was her mother's birth name.

Maureen's grandmother was widowed at an early age, when Mary Lewsley was just a babe in arms. Hence, Mary didn't have a father's love.

Widowhood, together with a struggle to survive, didn't allow Mary's mother the time to bestow the love that she felt towards her daughter.

Maureen recognised this emptiness in her mother, together with unfulfilled potential.

So, in honour and recognition of her mum, Maureen wanted her pen name to be Mary Lewsley.

Maureen spends her time between England and her second home in Ireland, which has inspired many of her stories.

Contents

1. The Roughty Bar 1
2. The Bakery 7
3. The Paper Shop 13
4. Molly's Cafe 19
5. The Book Shop 27
6. The Sweetie Shop 33
7. The Linen Shop 41
8. Saturday Night at the Roughty Bar 47
9. The Handshake 51
10. And The Rest is History 55
11. Being There 61
12. By Chance 71
13. David's Bus 77
14. Father Brown 81
15. My Easter Angel 89

16. The Bracelet.. 95
17. The Car Keys... 101
18. The Coat... 115
19. The Dressing Table 125
20. The Glass Teddy Bear............................. 135
21. The Mirror... 141
22. The Little Apple.. 149

1

The Roughty Bar

An overwhelming deathly silence pervaded the air. A heavy stillness hung in suspension, like a video on pause. Twenty-year-old ashes lay in the grate of the Roughty Bar. Pint glasses settled on tables; some still with beer, some without. A chair lay tipped on its back. It was the chair that had held the weight of the publican Johnny Finnigan when he took a fatal heart attack as many years ago as the ashes that lay in the grate. The hands on the clock were frozen at ten past the sixth hour – am or pm, no-one knows. It stopped when its minutes of life ran out after the last wind of the key by the hand of Johnny Finnigan.

Mary Finnegan was so distraught by the passing of her husband that she locked the bar and declared it would die with him. No-one was allowed in there. It became a shrine to his memory: a shrine that was never visited and respects never paid.

Over the years Mary's children pleaded with her to either re-open the bar or sell it. Mary insisted that in her lifetime she couldn't bear to see it resurrected in any way unless Johnny was resurrected too. As the latter was impossible, her children took this to mean a definite 'no'. Mary had three children – Finbar, Patrick and Sinead. Sinead was the youngest and a big believer in the power of prayer. She worried about her mammy and worried that not being able to open the bar nor let it go was taking its toll on Mary's health. Sinead decided she would offer up a Novena for her mammy to help her come to terms with dealing with the bar one way or another. Sinead felt if Mary could release herself from Johnny's shrine, it would enable her to move forward and have some future happiness, rather than be buried in the past like the room in the Roughty Bar.

Sinead could be seen each morning for the next nine days entering the church to recite her Novena to St. Anthony. She asked him to help her mother find herself again and find the strength to be able to delight in life being restored in the Roughty Bar.

The months went by and Sinead could see no difference in Mary. Her eyes were still lifeless and her spirit low. Finbar and Patrick had lost patience with their mammy, as they thought 20 years of grieving was just beyond a joke. They worked in the hotel trade in the next town and they would love nothing more than to see the Roughty Bar brought back to life. They were both competent chefs and putting their energies and skills into their own business would be a dream come true.

Johnny Finnegan had always brought his children up to respect their mammy, so the anger and resentment felt by the brothers filled them with guilt and had to be suppressed at the thought of what Da would say.

It was August and the summer cattle fair was in town – another reason for Mary Finnegan to cocoon herself in the past. Johnny Finnegan, although not a farmer, had always loved to take leave of his bar and wander into the square. Mary could still see him in her mind's eye, leaning on the tubular steel of the cattle pens, watching the antics of the traders. There were other market stalls in the town selling their wares, and several small caravans, with the owners competing against each other and all proclaiming that they could read your fortune.

Mary thought it would be the ideal day to light a candle for Johnny, despite having to battle her way through the many stalls and caravans to get to the church. Mary spent a good half hour in silent prayer and reflection. She relived some of the happy hours she had spent with Johnny. She left her candle burning brightly in front of the statue of St. Anthony and prayed the light would reach Johnny in heaven. She left the church and felt a sense of peace, something she hadn't felt for a long time. She smiled at stallholders and even passed the time of day, something else she hadn't done for a long time. Suddenly a small Romany-looking woman appeared from inside her caravan, right in the path of Mary.

"Hello darlin', would you not like me to tell your fortune?"

Mary looked into her dark black eyes and thought, *I don't have a future.*

The woman's glare was quite hypnotic.

"Things are not as bad as you think. Why don't you step inside?"

Mary could not believe her own actions. She had no belief in psychics or mediums of any description, yet before she knew it she found herself being guided, as if in a trance, into the little caravan that stood at the edge of the square. Half an hour later, Mary reappeared, a little ashen-faced, but with life back in her eyes. The medium had told Mary all about Johnny and how he had died. She said Johnny wanted to know why no-one was winding up his clock or visiting his bar. Mary felt a weight had been lifted from her that day, and as she thanked God that night, she knew what had to be done.

Her three children were summoned together on Sunday afternoon. Mary announced to Finbar and Patrick that she was handing the bar over to them on condition they made the best food in town. They could not believe what they were hearing, but they were all delighted and over the moon with the joyous news. There was no way Mary would tell them about the gypsy. She just explained herself by saying she'd had a change of heart.

First thing in the morning Sinead went into the church to tell St. Anthony the good news and thanked him for helping Mammy find herself.

2

The Bakery

Liam Kelly and Bridie Scanlon started the same school on the same day, both at the tender age of five years old. They were quite quiet and shy and went through school keeping themselves in the background. They were never in any drama group nor participated in any after-school sporting events. Ageing into adolescence didn't make either of them any more extrovert; they still retained their quiet and gentle personalities. I suppose 'contented' would sum them up very nicely. Both were happy to have left school to work in their family businesses.

Joe Kelly, Liam's father, owned and ran the wee bakery shop next door to the Roughty Bar. He rose very early each morning, apart from Sundays, to bake for the day ahead. Freshly baked bread permeated the little streets around and Joe was convinced the beautiful aroma was a wonderful mood enhancer for the early morning risers. Liam was becoming quite proficient at baking and even had some ideas for other baking products.

He also worked in the shop and the older female customers loved to be served by him. Liam was every mother's dream of a son-in-law. He had a gentle demeanour, a polite manner and a charming smile. Despite him having a quiet nature, it didn't hinder him having a sense of humour.

Bridie worked in her mother's café, which was located in the same wee row of shops as the bakery. Bridie would always make sure fresh flowers adorned the tables, along with crisp and clean red and white check tablecloths. She delighted in creating a beautiful space, giving pleasure for others to enjoy.

They say opposites attract, but this wasn't the case for Bridie and Liam. It was their similar gentle and charming personalities that drew them together and they loved each other's company. Ironically, it was their similar personalities that also kept them apart. They had fallen in love, but neither of them was brave enough to declare it to the other.

Every morning, Bridie would call at the bakers to pick up the order for the cafe. On the mornings Liam was serving in the shop, Bridie's face could light up a night sky. If for any reason Liam wasn't serving, Bridie's eyes were full of disappointment. Joe Kelly, being an observant man, knew what love looked like and he knew when he saw it. He definitely saw it between Liam and Bridie, but felt they needed a bit of a shove. Joe spent the weekend racking his brain, thinking how he could contrive to bring these two love birds together.

Monday morning came around and Joe was no further forward with his little scheme.

Jesus, he thought, *there must be something I can do.*

He went down into the kitchen to make his early morning cup of tea as he did every morning, apart from Sundays of course. His little ritual was to tear the previous day's date off the calendar and expose another new day.

"My God, is it the 7th February already? Christmas seemed like only last week."

"That's it, that's it, that is it!"

The penny had just dropped with Joe that this time next week would be Valentine's Day – the day when a young man could anonymously declare his love for another. Joe had now got the gist of his plan, but he had to work out how to put it into operation.

February 14th rolled around and Joe made absolutely sure that Liam would not be serving in the shop that morning when Bridie came in to collect her order for the cafe. The bell rang on the bakery door.

"Good morning Mr. Kelly."

"Good morning Bridie. It's a grand morning, is it not?"

"It is indeed. Just my usual order please, Mr. Kelly."

"There you go Bridie and I have a little bag here that Liam asked me to give ye."

Bridie looked puzzled as she walked back to the cafe. She went into the back room to open her little paper bag alone. She pulled out a beautiful heart-shaped biscuit with *'I Love You'* neatly iced across the middle. Bridie's face blushed; her hands were shaking and her heart beating like a drum.

That evening after dinner, Bridie sat down and carefully penned a little letter to Liam. It read:

Dear Liam,

Thank you so much for the wee Valentine's gift that you asked your Da to pass on to me. It made me so very happy. I hope you won't mind if I tell you I love you too.

Love always, Bridie

Next morning, with her legs like jelly and heart pounding, she made her usual call to the bakers. To her great disappointment, yet paradoxically her relief, Liam was not there. Bridie looked shyly at Joe and asked him if he would pass her letter on to Liam.

"Of course my dear. I'll be after having to charge you two postage."

He winked at her knowingly.

Joe passed Bridie's letter to Liam, who looked puzzled.

"Why would Bridie be writing to me Da?"

"Well how would I know? If you open it, you might find out."

With all his subterfuge, Joe could feel a visit to the confessional box imminent. Liam read the letter there and then; his questioning eyes looked up at Joe.

Joe explained everything. "Forgive me son, but it was so painful to watch you two so obviously in love. I just thought you could do with a wee hand."

Liam smiled his charming smile. "Thank you Da, I guess I did."

3

The Paper Shop

The shrill of that cheap alarm clock never failed to make its presence known on the sixth hour every morning. It was such an uncivilised and abrupt way to be woken from slumber. Tom O'Sullivan insisted that it was placed on the dresser out of reach of the bed. That way, his wife Annie had no choice, but to get out of bed to silence the little blighter and Tom would have no fear of oversleeping.

Tom was a tall obese man with big hands, fat fingers and a gruff voice. He controlled and bullied Annie, who was as small as he was large. Tom got out of bed when he could smell the odour of bacon rising up the stairs and seeping through the cracks of the bedroom door. He demanded tea and a bacon sandwich before releasing the locks to open up for the day.

Annie always obeyed his demands in her subservient manner. She had totally lost her identity, so much so that she was a stranger to herself. Her clothes were dowdy; she wore serviceable lace-up shoes and no make-up, all to the order of Tom O'Sullivan. He never made her feel special, nor displayed any affection towards her. Annie had given up trying to exchange humorous banter with him years ago, as he never saw the funny side and always replied in a bad-tempered manner. He lacked the ability to be self-deprecating, yet often used Annie as the butt of his jokes.

The jokes didn't start until he faced his audience. The curtains went back and Tom O'Sullivan stepped onto the stage when the doors of their paper shop opened. The chameleon had changed his colour. It was the only time he patted Annie on the shoulder, all being it was fake affection and part of the act. Annie's voice was drowned out. He finished her sentences and took over her stories. She felt suffocated. Customers thought he was great craic, but only Annie knew any different. She also knew she couldn't keep living these groundhog days without any happiness in her life. She felt she couldn't live in Tom's shadow any more, but her dilemma was that she didn't know how to get out of it.

When the shop closed at the end of the day, Tom would walk along to the Roughty Bar to partake in a glass of the black stuff, while Annie prepared dinner. She also took the opportunity to sit down with a cup of tea and luxuriate in five minutes to herself. She would sit in her rocking chair and dream that tomorrow might be different. The door leading to the hall was ajar and as Annie rocked away, she could see what looked like a piece of paper peeping out from under the dresser in the hall.

She got up to inspect it closer. It was a letter in a white window envelope addressed to her. She quickly opened it before Tom came home. It was from Murphy and Son, a firm of solicitors in Dublin. The letter was informing Annie she had been mentioned in the Will of Catherine Doyle. Catherine Doyle was her late father's spinster sister, whom Annie visited in her school holidays.

Annie heard Tom's heavy hand on the door handle. She quickly folded up the letter and buried it deep in her apron pocket. She thanked the Lord for it sliding under the dresser, as Tom vetted all the post and if anything was addressed to Annie, he opened it for her.

Sleep came late to Annie that night; her mind was going over and over, thinking about her letter, the logistics of making an appointment with the solicitor and physically getting there. As luck would have it, Murphy and Son had an office in Cork as well as Dublin. Cork was a lot nearer for Annie. Although with Tom breathing down her neck, it seemed a million miles away.

The next day, Mary Finnegan from the Roughty Bar went into the paper shop.

"Hi lads, I am organising a shopping trip to Cork for the ladies in the town. Could I trouble you to put this notice in your window?"

Before Annie had chance to reply, Tom O'Sullivan bellowed out,

"We can indeed, we can indeed."

"Oh thanks a million Tom. Annie, would you not come with us?" Completely out of character, Annie said she would love to go.

Holy name of Jesus, Annie thought, *someone up there is looking down on* me. *I can now go to Cork without composing a short story to tell Tom.*

When Mary Finnegan left the shop, Tom was fuming and told Annie not to expect any money from him to go shopping.

Next day, Annie phoned the solicitor and was praying she could get an appointment the same day as the shopping trip. Thank the Lord, it was no problem and it was all arranged.

The day came around and Annie was so excited to be travelling to the big city on her own. She had the solicitor's letter and all requested paperwork secured safely in her handbag. She felt Annie Doyle had returned. Her thoughts then turned to her Aunt Catherine. She couldn't think why she would be mentioned in her Will. The only thing she could think of was that she had been left the musical box that she used to play with on her visits to Aunt Catherine in the school holidays.

Annie arrived at the solicitor's office 15 minutes early. She nervously opened the door, announced herself to the receptionist and apologised for being early.

"That's ok Mrs. O'Sullivan. Please take a seat."

Ten minutes passed by and Liam Murphy stepped out of his office and greeted Annie O'Sullivan with a firm handshake.

"Please come in Mrs. O'Sullivan."

Annie emerged about an hour later, looking shocked, but with a spring in her step. Aunt Catherine had left Annie her beautiful Georgian house and the whole of her remaining estate, which amounted to a considerable amount of money. Annie couldn't wipe the smile from her face on the journey home, as she knew tomorrow morning she would silence that little blighter of an alarm clock one more time and Tom would not be smelling the smell of bacon seeping through the cracks in the bedroom door.

4

Molly's Café

Molly's cafe was as pretty on the inside as it was on the outside. Spring, summer, autumn and winter, the flowers and foliage in the hanging baskets complemented the shades of colour in the paintwork. It would entice anyone in for an early breakfast, a midday lunch, or afternoon tea.

Molly Scanlon remembers fondly when she and her husband Declan Scanlon first opened the doors of their little dream cafe. Declan always wrote the menu for the day on the large blackboard that was positioned in a place all the customers could read it. Molly insisted that Declan always chalked up the menu.

"Declan," she would say, "you have a beautiful hand."

Declan would smile affectionately at his wife. They had so much love for each other and that love was reflected in the food they served and in the ambience they created. All mortal souls who ate in Molly's cafe left happier than when they entered.

Molly and Declan longed for a child, but each month the dreaded visitor would make its unwelcome appearance, confirming once more that Molly had failed to conceive yet again. Despite their disappointments, they thanked God for what they did have and knew if it was His will, it would happen.

Spring through to autumn was the busiest of times in the café, so each January Molly and Declan would take themselves off to warmer climates for a well-earned respite from their hard, but enjoyable work.

However, this time they thought they would go to Rome and visit the headquarters of their faith. They prayed daily in many of the beautiful churches and lit numerous candles. They had a wonderful time and felt uplifted by their spiritual experience. What they didn't realise at the time was that two of them went to Rome, but three of them came back. Nine months later, Molly gave birth to a beautiful baby girl, whom they named Bridie after Molly's granny. Molly was told she wouldn't be able to have more children after Bridie. They had waited so long for Bridie, they felt very blessed to have her.

Bridie was a model child and a beautiful soul. She grew into a very kind and thoughtful young girl without a bad bone in her body, always helping out with the cafe when she could. When Bridie reached the age of 15, her father Declan fell ill and sadly died. Molly and Bridie were beside themselves with grief. Bridie held Molly tightly in her arms.

"I will look after you, Mammy. Meself and Granny can do extra hours and we can hire a new cook."

"You are a good girl Bridie. I don't know what I would do without you."

Molly insisted Bridie chalked up the menu each morning before she left for school. It was a really difficult time for Bridie, as she had more schoolwork than ever. She was not ambitious and wasn't really bothered about studying, but she felt it was expected of her. Bridie scraped through her exams with respectable passes. However, she decided emphatically there was to be no more studying for her.

On Sunday morning, after breakfast and before Mass, Bridie asked her mammy to sit down.

"Mammy, would you be annoyed with me if I didn't stay on any longer at school?"

"But Bridie, are you not happy there? Is someone bullying you?"

"No Mammy, no. Nothing like that. I just would love to work in the cafe full time. It's where I want to be. It's what I love doing."

"Well, if you are sure me darlin'. I would be delighted and your father would be too. Come and give me a hug before we miss Mass altogether."

Bridie loved her work with a passion and it showed in her meticulous attention to detail.

The weeks turned into months and before Molly and Bridie had noticed, a couple of years had escaped their attention. Life without Declan had been difficult, but they had learned to cope. It was a beautiful spring day and Bridie told her mammy she was off out for a Sunday afternoon walk in the park.

"Ok, Bridie love, enjoy your walk."

A few hours later, and later than Molly expected, Bridie returned home.

"I have something to tell you, Mammy."

"What is it Bridie, are you alright?"

Since Declan had died, Molly had become quite protective towards Bridie.

"I'm fine, Mammy. I just wanted to tell you I am seeing Liam Kelly from the bakery."

For a few fleeting moments Molly experienced that feeling of young love and she could see it in Bridie's face. Her eyes sparkled, her face glowed and her aura was encapsulated with happiness. Molly was overjoyed for Bridie, as Liam Kelly was the nicest young man in town and, as an added bonus, he was also very easy on the eye.

It was Christmas Eve and Bridie and Liam decided to go to Midnight Mass together. At the end of Mass, Liam suggested they lit candles and sat by the nativity crib to say a wee prayer. As they sat in prayer, Liam took Bridie's hand in his. He pulled a small, brown paper bag from his pocket and handed it to Bridie. She slid her hand out of his and carefully opened the bag.

"Oh Liam, you have baked me a biscuit, thank you."

"Well, I thought you might be hungry after Mass and with fasting all day." He laughed nervously.

Bridie pulled the biscuit from the bag to take a closer look. It seemed like Valentine's Day all over again, except this time the iced message on the biscuit read, *Will you marry me?*

Bridie blushed. "Oh Liam, I will. I will, of course. How beautiful of you to ask me in church."

"Well I thought I needed some support and who better to ask but the big man Himself?"

They giggled, hugged each other and walked out of church on cloud nine. Liam's Christmas present to Bridie was the most beautiful emerald engagement ring, her favourite stone.

After the hype and excitement of Christmas, Bridie and Liam's time was taken up focusing on the wedding. With both of them having quiet personalities, they were in agreement that they wanted a small wedding with immediate family and a few close friends. Bridie was adamant she wanted her mother to give her away.

After the cafe closed at the end of the day, Bridie and Molly would always sit down and have a cup of tea. Bridie placed her hand on top of Molly's.

"Mammy?"

"Yes Bridie. That sounds like you want something."

"Mammy, I would like you to give me away and make a wee speech at the wedding. Oh and if I give you the guest list, could you write out the invitations?"

Molly nearly choked on her tea.

"Are you ok, Mammy?"

"Yes Bridie I'm fine. My tea went down the wrong way."

Molly now had a huge dilemma. She had a secret, a secret she had never told anyone; not even her beloved Declan. She went to bed that night with enough thoughts to bring on insomnia for weeks. The next morning, Molly was still in turmoil over Bridie's wedding request.

Molly and Bridie always rose early so they could have a leisurely breakfast to set them up for the day. At breakfast this particular morning, Bridie produced a little package.

"Mammy, these are the invitations and here is the list of guests. So, can I leave that to you? It would be so helpful."

Molly sat and stared at the package with fear in her eyes. Tears rolled down her cheeks. Her body trembled.

"Mammy, what on earth is the matter?"

"Oh Bridie, I have something to tell you. Something I should have told you before. Something I should have told Daddy, God have mercy on him."

"Mammy what is it? What is it? You are scaring me now."

"Bridie love, I won't be able to write your invitations. What I should say is, I can't read or write. I can deliver a speech for you, as that will come from my heart, not my head. I don't need to write it down. I only ever learned to write my name. I'm so sorry Bridie."

"Mammy you mustn't apologise. I never realised, but now I know why you would never write up the chalkboard menu. You are never too old to learn, Mammy and I am going to make sure to find you a good teacher."

Molly hugged her daughter tightly.

"Do you know Bridie, I feel like I have had the heaviest of weights lifted from my shoulders. I feel free at last."

5

The Book Shop

Frances Darcy was passionate about books, especially second-hand books. She loved the musty smells and sensed the energies of readers gone before. Her little shop was an Aladdin's cave for literary lovers. There was a quiet corner with squidgy sofas and free coffee for anyone wishing to peruse before buying, or not. Gentle classical music played softly in the background, creating a calm, tranquil environment that would seduce anyone to want to stay all day.

Frances had a couple of local customers who were tempted on a weekly basis to call into her shop for a free cup of coffee. There was old Jim Murphy, who always paid a visit to the bookshop after his Friday visit to the butchers for his weekly sausage and bacon. Then there was Grace Foley, mother of Siobhan Foley from the Linen Shop. She came into town on Saturdays to pay her newspaper bill to Tom O'Sullivan. Although Tom was even more of a grump these days since Annie had left him, he never missed the opportunity to flirt with Grace Foley.

Grace didn't suffer fools gladly and in her eyes Tom O'Sullivan was a fecking eejit. If she wanted a man in her life in her advancing years, it certainly wouldn't be Tom O'Sullivan. Grace would make sure to place her money for her paper bill directly on the counter. She once had the skin-crawling experience of placing the money in Tom's fat fingers, only to have her hand crushed in his vice-like grip. With the unpleasantries over, Grace would make her way down to the Book Shop for a little read, a relaxing experience and a free coffee. Frances D'Arcy never minded Grace or Jim using her bookshop for their little sanctuary. Grace often donated the odd used book and Jim lived on his own so felt a bit lonely at times. It warmed Frances's heart to be able to provide a refuge for two of her dearest customers.

Frances had been adopted when she was six months old. She was an only child to her adoptive parents. When Frances was 12 years old, her parents explained to her that she was adopted and at the same time they gave her a beautiful pewter photo frame which held a photo of an attractive lady with shoulder length hair, a warm smile, yet sad eyes. Her parents explained to her how young her biological mother was when she gave birth to Frances and was forced to give her baby to the nuns before they later adopted her.

To say it was a shock to Frances was an understatement, but time as they say, is a great healer.

The beautifully framed photo was taken to the convent by Frances's birth mother some years after the adoption. She pleaded with the nuns to pass it on so that Frances would know what her mother looked like. There was one kind nun, Sister Veronica, who made sure the photo was delivered safely. Sister Veronica thought that if Frances's parents were happy to give her the photo, then that was all that mattered. Frances was delighted to have the photo, but always kept it locked away, occasionally taking it out to look into the deep sad eyes of her mother.

Wedding bells were never heard for Frances. It was far too late for her to have children, so why bother? she thought. Besides, she had never met anyone with whom she would want to spend the rest of her life. Frances loved her own company and relished her Sundays with a passion.

One particular Sunday she opened the drawer that housed her mother's photo. She often thought about her birth mother and wondered what path life had taken her. She ran her fingers around the frame and was mindful of its beauty. Frances never had a desire to find her birth mother, but was happy to know what she looked like. The more she admired the frame and looked into the sad eyes of her mother, she came to the realisation that this beautiful photo should be hung. For the first time she felt a closeness and connection to a mother she had never known, and felt she wanted to hang the photo for her. Frances gave a lot of thought as to where the photo would be hung and remembered there was a bare section of wall in the reading area of the bookshop. The frame would furnish it nicely.

Frances had an extra spring in her step on Monday morning. She felt a strange excitement about hanging her mother's photo. She was feeling a lot of love in her heart for her birth mother and was starting to reflect on her mother's life and understand the sadness in her eyes. Her mother's pain had become her pain. How Frances wished she could hug her mother and tell her she was ok.

As Frances unlocked her shop that Monday morning, she noticed that the old ceramic door knob had survived the many twists and turns of the thousands of visitors that had walked through its doors over the years. The busy tourist season had come to a close, but there was still a slow stream of autumn visitors. It was midday when a tall young man entered the shop, allowing the sound of the Angelus bell to follow him in. Frances was busy tending the coffee machine.

"Err, excuse me, but do you have any........." He stopped in his tracks and glared at the photo in the reading area.

Frances had noticed his glare and enquired if he was alright.

"Can I ask you if you know the lady in the photo?" he enquired.

Frances tried to act as naturally as possible. Her mind was working overtime as to know what to say.

"No. No, I don't know her. Why do you ask?"

"Well, believe it or not, but that's my granny."

Frances's voice went up an octave. "Your granny? And where is she now?"

"Next door. She runs the sweetie shop. I am down from Dublin visiting her."

"You mean Peggy Foley from the sweetie shop is your granny?"

"Yes, she moved down here some years ago with Granddad when he retired as a Guard. But Mum still lives in Dublin. Anyway, you must know all this. She loves reading."

"Yes, of course I know her and I am partial to pear drops."

"Are you ok? You look a little pale," he remarked.

"Thank you, I'm fine, I think I need a strong coffee with lots of sugar."

6

The Sweetie Shop

The pavement outside the sweetie shop was brushed to within an inch of its life morning, noon and night. Peggy Foley had an obsession with keeping her shop frontage clean and litter-free. Woe betide anyone she caught dropping litter and anyone meant anyone, from some mother's child to the parish priest. Her bark was worse than her bite. She loved to watch the little children with their weekly pennies of pocket money standing wide-eyed in bewilderment as to which sweeties to choose.

Peggy was born and bred in Dublin. At the age of 20, she married Gerard Foley, a 25-year old Guard. They started a family almost immediately and went on to have two girls and a boy. Peggy had a very happy marriage and her children meant the world to her. Yet inside her she carried a secret and a heartache that she had never shared, not even with her husband.

The 16-year old Peggy had become pregnant far too early in her little life. She was frightened, incredibly frightened. Her father was a devout, strict Catholic man. She knew he would see it as shame on the family. Peggy would stare at her father across the dinner table and shudder at the thought of telling him. She wore her blouse outside of her skirt until she could conceal her sin no longer. As predicted, her father was outraged. He made plans for her to be taken into the convent and let the nuns take over.

On 16th October Peggy gave birth to a little girl. Little did she know at the time, but Oscar Wilde's birthday was a very appropriate date for her daughter to be born, with her enormous love of literature. She knew her baby was going to be stolen from her. Her sorrow was immense. Each year on that date, Peggy would visit the church to say a prayer and light a candle for her daughter. She always wished she could light candles on her birthday cake.

When Gerard Foley took early retirement from the Guarda, he had a yearning to return to his native Kerry. He was proud of his three children. They had all come out of university with good degrees and were journeying on their own separate paths. Gerard thought he wouldn't be able to persuade Peggy, the city girl, to move to rural Kerry. When he told her there was a train from Killarney to Dublin, so she wouldn't have to always rely on him to drive her, she was happy. Peggy could drive, but would never have the confidence to make that long journey on her own.

Gerard was so looking forward to moving south. He was looking forward to relaxing and playing golf, his favourite pastime. Peggy on the other hand, wasn't prepared to be a golf widow and didn't feel quite old enough to retire completely.

They had been installed in their Kerry home for almost six months. The house was ship-shape and Peggy was getting itchy feet to get out and find herself a little job.

It was Friday evening and Gerard had returned home from the golf club. He asked Peggy if she would like to go to a dinner at the golf club the following weekend.

"I thought it might be a good opportunity for you to meet some new friends."

"Oh Gerard, that is kind of you. I shall look forward to that."

Saturday soon came around and Peggy was feeling quite excited. She had been off to Cork in the week and treated herself to the most beautiful peacock blue lace dress. Before leaving their house for dinner Gerard kissed his wife gently on the cheek and told her how beautiful she looked, as he always did.

The people at the golf club were friendly and made Peggy feel very welcome. After dinner Peggy and Gerard joined a quartet of other diners for drinks in the bar. There was Mabel and Tom and Collette and Tony. Collette in particular liked to find out as much as she could about a person when she was first introduced. She was curious to know how Peggy filled her time since moving down to Kerry. Peggy explained that now she had her house in order she would welcome a little job, maybe in a wee shop. Tony was earwigging as to what his wife was discussing. He never liked to miss a thing.

"Well, have you heard Pat Casey is looking for someone to take over his empty shop? He is not selling it, just wants someone to run it for him. He wants more time on the golf course," Tony piped up.

A week had passed by since the golf club dinner and Peggy Foley's thoughts were constantly preoccupied with the empty shop in town. She decided that after breakfast she would discuss it with Gerard. Pat Casey wasn't a stranger to Gerard. They had coupled up on the golf course a few times.

Gerard could see Peggy had given the shop a lot of thought and was quite serious about running it. He promised when he went to the golf course on Wednesday he would see Pat Casey and find out more about it.

On Wednesday afternoon Peggy's phone rang. It was Gerard.

"Peggy me darlin', could you meet me and Pat at his shop in an hour?"

Peggy was there exactly an hour later. The deal was done. All Pat wanted was for Peggy to pay a monthly rental and then she could treat the shop as her own. That was the birth of the sweetie shop.

Peggy had one grandson, Peter. He had been visiting his granny in the sweetie shop since he was almost a teenager. He would travel down from Dublin with his parents, full of excitement at the thought of helping Granny in her sweetie shop. He was now of an age where he could get the Dublin to Killarney train unaccompanied. His grandad would pick him up at the station and relate stories from his childhood on the journey back, most of which Peter had heard before, but loved to hear again.

Next morning, after a good night's sleep and one of Granny's full Irish breakfasts, Peter wandered into town. He told Peggy he was going to the bookshop, as he had never been before and he would meet up with her in the sweetie shop later.

"Ok me darlin', don't forget to bless yourself on the way out."

Peggy adored Peter and she was never happier than when he came to visit.

The door of the sweetie shop opened with an extra thrust.

"Granny, Granny, you will never guess what! That photo Mammy has of you when you were younger; well there is one hanging in the bookshop."

Peggy froze on the spot. She was paralysed from head to foot. When she thawed out sufficiently and loosened her muscles, she replied, "Well I did have two of them. Maybe that one made its way to the junk shop."

"What, all the way down to Kerry?" Peter laughed. "You must go and see it Granny."

The night was long for Peggy; sleep didn't come easy. The burning question searing through her mind was, *was Frances Darcy her daughter?*

Thursday was the anniversary of Peggy giving birth in the convent all those years ago. She relived every moment as if it were yesterday. Her sorrow was still as immense. After lighting her candle and saying a little prayer in the church, Peggy decided to call into the bookshop. She turned the old ceramic door knob. The bell on the back of the door rang out. Her hands were shaking, her legs trembling.

Frances looked up. Their gaze met. Without saying a word, the language in their eyes said everything.

Frances broke the silence. "Hello Peggy, would you like some cake? It's my birthday today."

"I know Frances. I know."

Tears rolled down Peggy's cheeks washing the sadness from her eyes.

Frances hugged her and said, "I'm ok Mammy, I'm ok."

7

The Linen Shop

It was such a pleasure to walk into the linen shop. Siobhan Foley liked to keep everything as white, bright and beautiful as the wedding dress she wore when she was jilted at the altar some 30 years ago by Frank Connelly, father to her unborn child. When the best man, Frank's brother Patrick Connelly, came into the church and handed Siobhan a letter, she had thought her world had ended. In his letter, Frank confessed he couldn't face the responsibility of fatherhood. He wished Siobhan a happy life, apologised and announced he was emigrating to America.

Seven months later, Siobhan delivered a beautiful baby boy into the world and christened him Sean Foley. She didn't think Frank Connelly had earned the right, respect, or privilege to give the baby his name. Siobhan knew it wasn't going to be easy bringing Sean up without a father. With the help and support of her mother and granny, she was able to keep her position as sales assistant in the local estate agents. The salary wasn't really adequate for someone in her circumstances, so she turned to her real love of dressmaking, to boost her income. She could make anything from kitchen aprons to wedding dresses. Her dream was to have her own little shop, with shelves of beautiful fabrics, boxes of buttons and counters adorned with linens and lace.

Siobhan worked from morn 'til night. She wanted the very best for Sean. She wanted him to be a decent person, knowing right from wrong. She hoped she could fulfil her own expectations of being a good parent without the guidance of a father. She worried, because her hours were long, that she might be neglecting spending time with Sean. She needn't have worried, as Sean thought the world of his mum. He was proud of her hard-working ethics. She inspired him with her wonderful creations.

From a small child Sean had been fascinated by the array of sewing aids and decorations, from pinking shears to sequins, all stored neatly in his mother's sewing room. He saw the delight in the eyes of her customers as they left her room clutching their completed garment. Sean had been so inspired by his mother, and also having a real flare for design himself, he went on to study fashion and design, eventually achieving the status of a leading fashion designer.

Siobhan sometimes had to pinch herself how her life with her son had turned out after being abandoned by Frank Connelly. Her world certainly hadn't ended as she thought it would on the day of her wedding. It had only just started. She had decreased her hours at the estate agency, so she could spend more time on her dressmaking. As good as Siobhan's skills were, her clientele was increasing on the back of Sean's success. Her dream of owning her own little shop was still her dream, but unless she landed an unexpected windfall she would have to keep on dreaming.

It was a Friday afternoon and Siobhan was clearing her desk for the weekend when she noticed details of a new sale instruction in her tray. She thought she would stay and get it typed up and photocopied. On close inspection, she saw that it was the end shop in the wee row of shops that was up for sale. That would suit Siobhan fine, but there was no way on God's earth she could buy it. Later that evening, Siobhan's thoughts were all-consuming. She couldn't get that little shop out of her mind and wondered if the owner would rent it to her.

After all, many of the other shopkeepers rent, she thought.

She rang Sean in Dublin to ask his opinion.

"Well Ma, are you sure? I know it's your dream. Owning a shop is one thing, but finding the rent every month is completely different."

Siobhan came off the phone realising her dream would always be just a dream. *Sean is right*, she thought.

Siobhan still kept a set of the shop details in her desk drawer, and when she had five minutes, she imagined how she would furnish it. She was actually daydreaming about her little shop when Mr. Kelly, the estate agent, called out to her.

"Siobhan, would you put a 'sold' sign on the details in the window. The details of the end shop in the wee row of shops. Thanks a million."

Even though she couldn't afford it, her heart sank.

She opened the curtains to a new day and decided to count her blessings and start focusing on Christmas, which was only three weeks away. Sean would be home and she loved to hear all about the craic in the fashion world. They normally went to Midnight Mass at Christmas, but Sean said he was feeling tired and suggested they go to early Mass on Christmas morning.

After Mass they walked arm-in-arm through the town to Sean's granny. She was preparing a lovely Christmas lunch with all the trimmings. Suddenly Sean stopped. He handed Siobhan an envelope.

"But what's this?" She looked puzzled.

"It's your Christmas present Ma. Open it."

There, inside the envelope, was a key with a beautiful satin bow tied to it and a little note which read:

Happy Christmas Ma.

Thank you for all you have done for me.

Now it is time for me to do something for you. This is the key to your little dream.

Love always, Sean.

8

Saturday Night at the Roughty Bar

It was another Saturday night at the Roughty Bar. Johnny Finnegan's clock had been rewound. His sons, Finbar and Patrick, were busy in the kitchen creating the tastiest of meals. Mary and Sinead Finnegan were waiting on tables and Mary at last had life in her eyes and a smile on her face.

The wee row of shops had shut their doors for the weekend. Their keepers would patronise The Roughty Bar over a relaxing meal and partake in a drink or two as a well-earned reward for a busy week.

The two most comfortable chairs by the fire were occupied by Bridie and Liam Kelly from the bakery and Molly's Cafe. Bridie and Liam had been happily married for 12 months, and in six months' time, God willing, they will be blessed with their first little bundle of joy.

When Bridie received confirmation that she was pregnant, she asked Liam's Da, Joe Kelly, to bake her a heart-shaped biscuit. On no account must he mention it to Liam. Bridie carefully iced the biscuit with a message that read "I'm pregnant", then placed it on the saucer of Liam's evening cup of tea. To say he was over the moon with excitement would be an understatement.

Perched on a high stool at the bar was Tom O'Sullivan from the paper shop. His big hands and fat fingers clutched his pint of the black stuff. He was fonder of drinking than eating now that Annie had left him. He'd an arrangement with Bridie from the cafe to have a bacon sandwich delivered around 10 each morning, when the rush for newspapers was over. Making himself a bacon sandwich was not a notion that would enter Tom O'Sullivan's head.

Molly Scanlon, Bridie's mother from the café, would be joining her daughter and Liam later. She was coping much better with life. It was a bitter sweet time leading up to her becoming a granny. It made her so happy, yet so sad that Declan would never get to see their grandchild.

Molly had been having lessons and was now able to read and write. She had become a frequent visitor to the book shop.

The Roughty Bar always had live music over the weekend and on Saturday nights the band was joined by a young singer, Deidre. Her voice was as soft as the breeze and as sweet as honey. Frances D'Arcy, from the book shop, loved to sit by the musicians. As well as her love of books, she also had a great love of music.

Frances had always been a loner. She felt content in her own skin until she met her mother, Peggy Foley, from the sweetie shop. It was then that she realised she had never really felt complete. Fate had dictated their paths crossed. This enabled her to meet and hug her mother and tell her she was ok. Frances felt real contentment like she had never felt before.

Peggy and her husband Gerard Foley liked to indulge in a nice meal of steak, chips and all the trimmings. Peggy would glance across at Frances and acknowledge her, as she did with other friends, but there was always love and affection in her eyes when she looked at Frances. Needless to say, it was reciprocated. Frances had told Peggy she wanted to let sleeping dogs lie. She didn't want anyone to know she was Peggy's daughter. Frances had never wanted siblings and she wanted it to stay that way.

Siobhan Foley from the linen shop, also had a love of music and, if space permitted, would sometimes join Frances D'Arcy and together they would enjoy the haunting sound of Deidre.

Siobhan's linen shop was still as white, bright and beautiful as the wedding dress she had been jilted in. Like the musicians, she was happy spending her time creating. Seeing the happiness in the eyes of her customers was an extra bonus.

The Roughty Bar was in full swing. Even folk from the next town would frequent on a Saturday night. Looking around, there were faces laughing, voices singing, stories exchanging and folk enjoying the craic. Looking closer, deep behind most of their eyes, there was sadness and sorrow. Inside, their hearts were bruised.

Come Monday morning, the wee row of shops will put their best feet forward. Their keepers will open their doors to the world and hide their sorrows from all that enter.

9

The Handshake

The night was dark; the whistling of mating deer could be heard in the distance. Deidre O'Sullivan lay and listened as her husband Tommy seemed to be competing as he lay in a drunken stupor. Competing only with the whistling, as there had been no mating in their bed for many a year. Deidre lay thinking about some of the lads in the town that she could have married.

I could have done better, she thought. *I could have done better.*

Her thoughts in particular went to Joe Darcy. As teenagers Joe had a soft spot for Deidre and always made a beeline for her at the Dance Hall on a Saturday night. Poor Joe never got as much as a glance from Deidre unless he invited her to dance. It was Tommy on whom she lavished her attention.

Her thoughts were interrupted abruptly as Tommy expelled one enormous fart.

Holy Mother of God, how did I get lumbered with this bloody eejit?

On that note, Deidre closed her eyes and hoped she would find some happiness in her dreams.

As the years had passed by in Deidre's marriage, Tommy O'Sullivan had not turned out to be the man she had thought. It would be kind to describe Tommy as a content and easy-going man, but the truth be known he was a total sluggard, set in his ways with not a thought for anyone but himself. Deidre, on the other hand, was a home-maker. She had drive and determination and by God she was a hard worker. She had energy by the bucketful and anything that was done in the house, or indeed in their life, was instigated by her.

Deidre was woken by the smell of stale alcohol and the occasional belch spewing out of Tommy's mouth.

Jesus, she thought, have *I really been married to this idle fecker for 50 years next month?*

Before she was totally asphyxiated, Deidre peeled her warm body off the mattress and made her way downstairs to start breakfast.

Tommy opened his eyes and rolled his tongue around his mouth to take away the dehydration symptoms of a hangover. He could smell the aroma of bacon escaping from the kitchen. He rolled his fat arse off the mattress, had a good scratch and made his way downstairs.

"Is there any of that left for me? I could murder a bacon sandwich."

Deidre put two slices of bacon between some bread and slapped it down in front of him.

"Do you know Tommy it is our Golden Wedding anniversary next month?"

"Is it indeed? How many years is that then?"

Deidre had a Damascus moment. She knew this was to be a sudden turning point in her life. Tommy's response to Deidre confirmed to her that he couldn't give a shit if they had been married for 10 or 50 years. She knew he wouldn't acknowledge it at all and certainly there would be no present of gold.

Well, she thought, *if Tommy won't surprise me, I will just have to surprise him.*

Deidre spent the next month planning and plotting.

It was Saturday morning and the big day had arrived. Deidre waited until breakfast was over.

"Tommy, our Golden Wedding anniversary is today and I would like to give you something to mark the occasion. Could you stand up please?"

Tommy rose from his chair, wiping the bacon grease off his mouth onto his shirt sleeve.

"Jesus woman, do I have to?"

Deidre held out her hand. "Shake hands with me Tommy."

"For feck's sake woman. Do I have to?"

He reluctantly shook her hand. "What's this all about Deidre?"

"It is my present to you, to mark our anniversary."

"A handshake?"

"Yes Tommy, a Golden handshake, for our Golden Wedding anniversary. I am leaving you on the very same date as I married you. Enjoy your present Tommy. I know I will."

10

And The Rest is History

It was a misty autumn morning as Marjory Roberts sipped her coffee and looked out of her window. She saw little piles of wet, yet colourful leaves, carpeting her lawn and bushy shrubs still trying to display their fading beauty.

"What shall I do today?" she asked herself. Her life was somewhat lonely, as she had lost her husband Peter three years ago. She was an only child and never had children of her own. She was in a reflective mood, almost bordering on regret: regrets regarding her childless marriage and her total devotion to Peter, to the exclusion of friends. She felt that now, in her early retirement, a circle of friends would be very welcome.

Her thoughts were abruptly interrupted by the heavy delivery of the morning post. *Oh good*, she thought, *that's my magazine.* She liked to read the Lonely Hearts column and fantasise that she might just send a reply and meet a soul mate: a friend, a companion, who shared her deepest thoughts and recognised her needs. However, it was only a fantasy, as Marjory was far too cautious and timid to follow her impulse and send a reply.

Oh dear, she thought as she glanced at the clock. It was 10am. The breakfast dishes lay cold in the sink and her bright blue fleecy dressing gown draped her bony shoulders. *Come on Marjory*, she told herself sternly, *get your chores done and make yourself look respectable.*

Half an hour later, she appeared in her sitting room looking prim and proper in her white blouse, navy cardigan and pleated skirt. Picking up her magazine, she settled into her favourite armchair and decided to indulge herself reading its varied content. As always, she read it from cover to cover. As she turned the page to the 'where are you now?' section, she heaved a sigh, her low self-esteem blocking any thought that anyone would be trying to trace her. Nevertheless, she liked to read it.

As her eyes moved quickly up and down the columns of names, they stopped sharply, blinked rapidly, and then transformed into a fixed stare. The words jumped out at her; she read it again and again. "Oh my God, I don't believe it. I don't believe it!" she cried. Someone was asking about her father, or rather someone with the same name as her father. This man had served in the

Royal Signals in Italy in 1943, as her father did. She was utterly speechless.

Placing her magazine on the table, she walked into the kitchen to make another coffee. Her thoughts were racing. *Is it my dad they are looking for? Who is this person? Why are they looking for him?* Her lonely empty life heightened her emotions; she felt anxious and excited all at the same time.

Later that afternoon, Marjory felt calmer, more focused. She had been to the corner shop to buy a notepad and envelopes. She had decided to respond to the mystery person in her magazine. She had to know if it really was her dad that they were looking for and why.

The leaves crunched under her highly polished boots as she walked nervously to the post-box. Her hand hesitated as she lifted her letter to the mouth of the box. Finally dropping it in, she heard the vacant sound of a recently emptied box and whispered, "I've done it."

Several weeks passed, and needless to say, each morning Marjory waited, eagerly anticipating the morning post. Then one Friday morning, hidden amongst the junk mail, was a hand-written envelope.

Her heart beating strongly, she delicately picked up her brass letter opener and neatly opened the envelope. The letter read:

Dear Marjory,

Thank you for your most welcome letter.

I do believe that it was your father who was a very good friend of my father when they served together in Italy.

My father spoke about your father with much affection and always wanted to find him after the war. Sadly, my father died recently, but I have some photos that you may like to see.

Would you believe, we only live 10 miles apart?

With kind regards,

Hilary

Hilary had included an e-mail address. Hurriedly, Marjory turned on the computer which previously had been used mainly by her husband.

After exchanges of e-mails, Marjory and Hilary decided to meet in a village pub, about halfway between their homes.

It was a frosty sunny morning, as Marjory woke to an exciting day. Today she had a purpose; she felt light and even looked younger.

Her thoughts were racing again. *I hope I will like Hilary. Will she be easy to talk to?*

Marjory arrived at the pub ten minutes early, as Marjory would. She had told Hilary she would wait inside the front door, as she was too nervous to sit in a pub on her own.

Suddenly she felt a soft tap on her shoulder. As she turned, there stood a tall, distinguished, grey-haired man.

"Sorry," she said. "Am I in your way? I'm waiting for a friend."

The man smiled kindly and said, "Are you Marjory?"

"Yes. Yes, I am, but... but... couldn't Hilary make it?"

He smiled again reassuringly and said, "I am Hilary."

The rest, as they say, is history.

11

Being There

Maria McCarthy was born in Birmingham to Irish Catholic parents. Her mother Ellen McCarthy, nee Guinney, came from Belfast in the north of Ireland and her father Joseph McCarthy came from rural Kerry. The couple met at a mutual friend's wedding in Dublin and were married 12 months later.

It was difficult enough in the early fifties to find employment in Kerry, let alone raise a family. Ellen and Joseph thought long and hard before deciding to move to England, where Maria was born 18 months later, on Christmas Day. It had been difficult for Ellen to conceive and she always maintains that Maria was God's gift to them.

When Maria was growing up, she was taken to Ireland many times, as she had grandmothers in the north and south. She loved to visit her granny in Belfast and go with her to St George's Market, where her granny would insist on tasting the cheeses before buying. Maria's granny would send her to the corner shop for messages. Maria had never heard of messages in that context. She can still remember the first time she went for messages; her granny had asked her to get scallions and sarsaparilla. Maria had no idea what she was talking about until her mother translated it for her into spring onions and lemonade.

Her visits to Kerry were quite different, but just as enjoyable. Her Granny McCarthy lived in a little grey house in the mountains, with no running water. Maria was always sent into the yard with a bucket to fill from the water pump. It was quite hard work for her; she would pump the handle up and down until her bucket was full and her arm ached. Maria loved to be in Ireland. She loved the people, the beauty and the relaxed way of life.

When Maria was in her late teens, both her grandmothers died within a week of each other. She was devastated. Maria and her parents set off to drive to the ferry to attend both funerals. Maria thought it was a lot of driving for her father, as they had to drive from north to south.

Maria went on deck as the ferry pulled out of the harbour. She reflected on all the times she had made this journey and remembered the excitement she had always felt at the thought of seeing her grannies. Her sadness was overwhelming and the realisation that she wouldn't see her grannies again and that it would be a long time before visiting Ireland was too much to bear.

After the funerals, Maria returned to England grieving not only for her grannies, but for her beloved Ireland too.

In the years that followed, Maria threw herself into studying. She graduated from university, qualified as a vet and joined a local practice. Within months, she met and was dating Bernard Wilson, a lovely young man from a neighbouring veterinary practice. Bernard was quiet and very easy going – just Maria's cup of tea. They had been dating for about 12 months when Bernard proposed. Maria was delighted. She told Bernard she didn't want a big fussy wedding; he was entirely happy with that. However, she did tell him she wanted their honeymoon to be in Ireland. Bernard thought Ireland could be rather cold or wet, but Maria insisted.

"I have so much to show you, so much I want to share with you. I feel like I am going home."

Bernard submitted to her wishes, especially when he saw the passion in her eyes.

To Maria, her wedding was a formality. She just wanted to get it done and dusted and become Mrs. Wilson. However, the honeymoon was a completely different kettle of fish. Her tummy churned with excitement, just like when she was that little girl who used to visit her grannies in the north and south of that beautiful Emerald Isle.

The wedding was quite understated, but Maria and Bernard were very content with that. They were happy and that's all that mattered to them. Bernard, however, still had reservations about going to Ireland, but for Maria's sake he kept this to himself. Wouldn't a flight to somewhere warm and sunny be preferable to a choppy ferry to Ireland, which potentially could be cold and wet? After all, it will be early October.

They decided to visit the north first and Maria took Bernard to all the places that her granny had taken her. It was a bitter sweet time for Maria, but she was so happy to be able to share her memories with her new husband and Bernard was beginning to see just why she was in love with this country. It was easy for Maria to show Bernard around Belfast, as she remembered the names of places and streets. It was a bit more difficult in the south because it was so rural. When Maria used to come with her father, she would sit in the back of the car while he drove through mountain passes and country lanes until they reached her granny's house. It didn't have a road name, or landmark; it was just there, halfway up a mountain.

There had been no need for Bernard to worry about weather conditions, as they were experiencing a beautiful Indian summer. Bright red fuchsias cascaded over grey stone walls along the roadside and bright orange montbretia complemented them beautifully, all brought together by the lush green ferns, some of which were starting to turn a soft pinky bronze.

Bernard was so happy that Maria had suggested Ireland for their honeymoon. He had fallen hook, line and sinker for its beauty and relaxed way of life. He understood now how she loved and missed this place. He was beginning to realise he could also call this place home, despite only being there for a short time. It was truly magical.

The couple were staying in a luxurious Victorian hotel near Killarney. It was so peaceful and stood beside the lake. The early morning autumn mist lay softly around the mountain as Bernard gazed in amazement at the beauty that lay before him. He walked over to Maria and held her in his arms.

"Thank you for bringing me to paradise. How could I ever have doubted your judgement?" They hugged each other gently; there was no need for words.

After breakfast, Maria and Bernard filled the car with petrol and explored the lanes of Kerry. Driving was a joy, as they virtually had the roads to themselves and on the rare occasions they met a car or a person, a friendly wave was always exchanged. All Maria could remember about her visits as a young girl were the towns she visited, like Sneem, Kenmare and Killarney. Somewhere in the surrounding mountains, her granny's house lay hidden.

Driving along the coast, they took a road to the right which climbed up into the hills.

"There doesn't look to be many houses up here," Bernard exclaimed.

"Well, there aren't many houses anywhere," said Maria. "That's the beauty of it all." As they turned around the next little bend in the winding lane, a 'For Sale' sign appeared in the hedge. They stopped the car to have a better look.

"Is there really a house under all that ivy?" Bernard said.

"Yes," Maria replied. "You can't see what the house looks like, can you?"

They got out of the car and Maria noticed a waterfall opposite.

"Bernard!" she cried. "This waterfall, I remember it from visiting my granny's house, but I can't recognise the house." Maria promptly opened the garden gate and ran round into the yard.

"Yes, it's here, Bernard, it's here."

"What's here?" shouted Bernard, as he ran to keep up with her.

"The pump, the water pump, where I used to fill my granny's bucket. Bernard, we have found my granny's house."

Tears of happiness rolled down Maria's cheeks and she couldn't talk of anything else on their way back to the hotel.

Next morning, Bernard told Maria he needed to talk to her. He had slept on his thoughts from the previous day and was pretty sure he was serious about the outcome.

Bernard had asked the hotel if they could prepare a packed lunch and suggested to Maria they had a picnic at the side of the lake. Maria thought it was a lovely idea. She took Bernard's hand and gave it a little squeeze to acknowledge his thoughtfulness. They picked up their picnic, packed in a lovely wicker basket and walked slowly down to the lake.

"Maria," Bernard said gently, "how would you like to live in Ireland?"

"Like to live here? Like to live here? I would love to live here, but I never thought in my wildest dreams that you would want to."

"Well, neither did I until I came here. It has seduced me, captivated me, thoroughly stolen my heart and I submit, I submit, I submit. I want to live here Maria, with you and your childhood memories. I want to make memories of our own and a good way to do that would be to buy your granny's house and refurbish it."

Maria was totally speechless and when she finally came down to earth she hugged and kissed Bernard until he couldn't breathe.

"You really have given this a lot of thought, haven't you? Thank you so much."

Down at the lake, the sun was setting and the autumn air was becoming chilly. Maria and Bernard strolled back to the hotel hand-in-hand. Tomorrow was another day.

The estate agent's office was small. Maria nervously pushed open the door. Although it had been her granny's house, she had no idea who owned it now. It transpired the house had been empty since her granny died and had been handed down to her father's brother, Maria's uncle, as he was the eldest son. Maria's father was aware of this, but had never mentioned it to her. However, her uncle had died recently, so the house had been left to his son, James, who was living in America. Although he was sad to be selling the house after it had been in the family for generations, he knew it was the sensible thing to do. James would love to see it bought back to life and loved again.

Mr. Foley, the estate agent, was delighted when Maria told him about the connection she had with the house. He also knew James from old, as they had been at school together. He knew James wouldn't want it to go to anyone else.

"Jesus Maria, that's a powerful story!" Mr. Foley exclaimed. "I will ring James tonight and give him the good news. He will be delighted, delighted, so he will."

Maria and Bernard walked out of the estate agents on cloud nine. "Do you know what Bernard?"

"No Maria, I don't know what. Tell me." He gave her a little squeeze.

"I think my grannies guided us to our little grey home in the West."

"Do you know Maria, I think you are right."

As they sailed back to England full of excitement and promise for their future, Bernard turned to Maria and asked, "What is it that you like most about Ireland?"

Maria looked at Bernard, smiled and said, "Being there Bernard. Just being there."

12

By Chance

The small Catholic school stood in the mist on a cloudy day and the smell of a nearby factory hung in the air like yesterday's washing. Mary Quinn was a pupil there; she was shy, quiet and very kind. She was extremely caring and protective to the children from less fortunate families. She befriended them at playtimes, as most of the other children thought they were dirty and smelly and not worth bothering with. Mary had a quiet confidence; she was always a leader, never a follower and was a good influence. This came across more when she moved up to senior school. She was bright and excelled at most subjects. It was Mary's plan to go to university. It was not her plan to meet a boyfriend at school at such an early age.

John Parker and Mary became inseparable. What Mary didn't realise was that John was becoming rather possessive. He wanted to know what her movements were and constantly wanted to be with her. Mary thought he was really sweet and was even flattered that he wanted to lavish so much attention on her.

Mary and John married when they were 18 years old. She didn't get to university and settled for a life of motherhood and domesticity, which she was happy with. Everything Mary did, she did it well. However, John's possessive, jealous, controlling nature had become much worse and was wearing her down. It was so bad now that he would undermine her at every possible opportunity. That bright, self-confident young girl was now a shadow of her former self. He was constantly telling her that she was ugly and skinny, so much so that she actually believed him. He would belittle and contradict her when she tried to tell the children the importance of study.

John wanted the best of both worlds. He liked to live it up, go to nightclubs, have affairs, yet wanted a wife at home to cook and clean. He had achieved what he wanted. Mary had been stripped of her self-esteem and her confidence had been destroyed. She trembled when she heard his car on the drive, wondering what his temper would be like. She always made sure she had her make-up on, hoping he wouldn't tell her she was ugly.

Fifteen years had now passed by and Mary's situation was no better; in fact, it was worse. She was so unhappy and depressed. Despite her lack of confidence, she knew she had to leave. She always thought she had to stay in her marriage for the children, but now she knew she had to leave for the children. Mary was in employment now, so she had a small income. She managed to rent a house nearby, despite it leaving her penniless and overdrawn at the end of each month.

What peace she felt as she put the key in her own front door. She had found her own little sanctuary for herself and her children. Her evenings were spent playing all the classical music she had missed so much. Mary wasn't wealthy, but she was rich. She was rich in knowing she wasn't frightened in her own home, rich in being able to do what she wanted to do, when she wanted to do it and rich in not having to be accountable for her every move.

With every new day that passed in Mary's new-found home, she was feeling more alive, more like herself of old. She wanted to do something creative, as her creativity, along with her self esteem, had been flattened.

I know what I can do, she thought. *I can write short stories in the evening when the children are in bed.*

Mary had quite a good imagination and within six months she had completed her first book of short stories. Writing them was one thing, but getting them published was quite another. She had two rejections from publishers. Though this was disappointing, she decided to give it a third attempt. The weeks turned into months and Mary had resigned herself to the fact that another rejection was on the way.

It was a late autumn evening. The phone rang.

"Hello, is that Mary Parker?"

"Yes, I am Mary Parker. Who's calling please?"

"Mrs. Parker, my name is Thomas Grant from Simpsons Publishers. If you remember, you submitted a collection of short stories."

Mary's heart was leaping out of her chest.

"Well, I have to be honest with you, I can't say I care for short stories myself, but by chance I took them home, as my wife is very fond of short stories. Anyway, I will get to the point and that is to say she thoroughly enjoyed them. So I am willing to publish them."

Mary was frozen to the spot; she was speechless.

"Hello, Mrs. Parker, are you still there?"

"Oh yes Mr. Grant, I am here. I can't believe it," Mary stuttered.

"Well, I can assure you it is true. I presume you are writing under the name of Mary Parker?"

"Yes, that's correct," Mary replied. "No, no wait. I would like to write under the name of Mary Quinn. After all, that's who I used to be; that's who I am."

13

David's Bus

Did our lives really happen?

Where did they go?

They went far too fast.

These were the thoughts of Sylvia Hunt as she walked up the shady path of the care home.

In her previous life, she had been happy, planning, looking forward to. No deep thoughts of the future. Only the present. Only the now. Her days were light, carefree and contented. Today they felt like solid matter, heavy with burdens and fears of the future. Her thoughts continued.

Where is that lovely young woman? I am sure she is still part of me, I just can't find her.

She pressed the buzzer on the door of the care home, otherwise known as Pastures New. Even the name made her feel nauseous and put a knot in her stomach. She was there visiting her husband, David. He had been taken over by that dreadful monster of a disease known as dementia. He didn't recognise her any more. He looked at her with empty eyes and complained to her that Sylvia didn't come to see him any more. She couldn't understand how he remembered who she was by name, but her face was lost somewhere deep in the shadows of his mind.

She found the visits utterly heart-breaking. Friends suggested she shouldn't visit, as David didn't know her. But Sylvia always reminded them that she knew him and loved him still.

Right from being a boy, David had always loved buses. He enjoyed nothing more than to go with his mother into Birmingham city on the number 15B bus. That was back in the 1950s, so buses looked a little different then. He would sit in wonder and observe every little detail. Sometimes he liked to sit at the front on the left. He could see the driver's cab from there. It was totally separate from the rest of the bus. He was absolutely fascinated by it, right down to the horizontally pleated blind that hung behind the driver. He would watch the conductor press the dark red bells that were strategically placed around the walls of the bus. How he wished he could press one, but that was strictly the conductor's job. David was intrigued by the various signs and receptacles, from the 'No

Spitting' sign to the 'Used Tickets' bin on the platform.

Despite his memory loss, he still remembered everything about that number 15B bus that he rode on so often.

Sylvia nearly always found David rearranging the chairs in the care home into two straight lines. This was David's bus. He would pretend he was a bus conductor, which in David's mind he was. Sylvia became his passenger. He asked her where she was going and gave her an imaginary ticket from his imaginary ticket machine. She would humour him with affection. She would give him pretend money and take her pretend ticket. She hated leaving him, but used her pretend bus journey as a kind way to end her visiting time.

"I have to get off at the next stop please."

That made David happy, as he could press his imaginary bell.

"Ding dong," he would say.

His eyes would search Sylvia's face, he would get agitated. She thought that he looked at her as if he remembered he had forgotten who she was.

"David," she said out of frustration. "How can you remember you have forgotten me, when you don't even remember I ever existed?"

David looked at her blankly and continued to drive his imaginary bus.

Each visit thereafter saw David becoming weaker and weaker.

It was Saturday night and Sylvia received a call from the care home.

"Mrs Hunt, we think you should come to see David. He has taken a turn for the worse."

Sylvia was at David's bedside at nine o'clock. She sat down quietly at the side of his bed, covered him with his cotton blanket and placed his hand in hers.

"I'm here David," she whispered.

He opened his eyes and focused his gaze on her face. He smiled and calmly said, "I think we have reached the terminus. Everybody off."

14

Father Brown

It was Sunday morning and Jim and Theresa Metcalfe attended 10 o'clock Mass as they did every Sunday at the Roman Catholic Church of the Sacred Heart, accompanied by their four-year-old son Anthony. Their faith was so important to them; they never took life for granted and always counted their blessings. Jim performed the duty of the collection plate and Theresa arranged flowers in the church. She was known for her artistic flower displays. The parish priest John Murphy was a very kind and gentle man, but sadly his health was failing. He was very fragile and his mobility was becoming suspect. He had more than fulfilled his duties to the Sacred Heart over the years and it was now time for him to relax in pastures new.

The church social committee had arranged a farewell party for Father Murphy and at the same time an introduction to the new parish priest, Father Dominic Brown. Cakes were baked, sandwiches discussed, grass was cut and the

Parish Hall decorated. A little army of parishioners had worked tirelessly for the big day. Jim and Theresa arrived early in order for Theresa to decorate the tables with miniature flower displays. Everything was perfect.

After the speeches and gift presentations people started to mingle and chatter. The main topic of conversation was "Where is Father Brown?" Everyone was anxious to meet him, to make their introductions and let him know of their importance in the parish. Suddenly the door opened.

"Ah, there you are!" exclaimed Father Murphy. "Come in Dominic. Come on in and meet your new parishioners."

"I am so, so sorry I am late. The traffic was horrendous."

"Not to worry, not to worry. You are here now," replied Father Murphy with understanding in his voice.

Theresa was serving tea at the top of the hall. Her friend Martha was a lot more inquisitive than Theresa and had gone down to meet Father Brown. She returned ten minutes later clutching Father Brown by the arm.

"Theresa," she cried, "let me introduce you to our new priest, Father Brown."

Theresa looked up from her enormous teapot. What happened next was not what she had expected. As their eyes met, their gaze was fixed. A light went on. There was a spark, an attraction, a magnetism, an excitement that she had never felt before.

"N-n-nice to meet you Father Brown. Would you like a cup of tea?"

As Jim and Theresa drove home, Theresa couldn't get Father Brown out of her mind. *This is so ridiculous*, she thought. *Why is this man in my head when I didn't even know him two hours ago?*

The alarm went off at 7.30am giving Jim and Theresa plenty of time to get ready for 10am Mass. There were no empty seats that Sunday. Even parishioners who didn't go to Mass regularly were intrigued to see how Father Brown would perform.

As the time came for Communion, Theresa's heart was thumping. *This is so wrong*, she thought. *I am receiving Communion, yet all I can think of is the priest.* Theresa said a quick Act of Contrition as she stood in line to receive the Holy Sacrament. As she placed her palms outstretched, their eyes met fleetingly yet meaningfully. Her guilt was all-consuming.

As the days and weeks went by, Theresa and Father Brown came in contact, but always with other members of the various church groups. The attraction between them was getting stronger and both of them wished it wasn't there. They communicated through the unspoken word; just a knowing look between them. Theresa did think about pulling out of all the church groups and the flower arranging, but why would she? She loved it and how would she explain it to Jim? She decided she would have to keep everything as normal. She hoped and prayed her feelings toward Father Brown would gradually lessen.

It was Friday afternoon and the church was closed. Theresa was allowed to have a key to the side door. There was a wedding on the Saturday and Theresa had a very big flower display assignment. The bride wanted flowers everywhere and she knew how talented Theresa was at arranging, as the bride herself was a parishioner of the church.

Theresa was working away when the door to the sacristy opened. It was Father Brown. Theresa blushed as her heart skipped a beat.

"Hello Theresa."

"Hello Father Brown. I am getting the flowers prepared for the big wedding tomorrow."

"Yes and I have to say you are doing a wonderful job."

"Oh thank you Father Brown, so nice of you to say so."

"It looks like you have nearly finished. Would you like to come over to the house and join me in a cup of tea?"

"Are you sure?" Theresa replied shakily.

"Yes Theresa, I am."

That Friday's afternoon cup of tea became the first of many cups of tea and Father Brown had now become Dominic. Their attraction for each other had got stronger until they couldn't resist each other any more. The deed had been done; a commandment had been broken. They were both in turmoil. A turmoil neither of them could control nor believe was happening to them.

Theresa's body ached when she wasn't with Dominic, yet she still had to lead a normal life with Jim. She couldn't hurt Jim. She didn't hate him; he was a good man, but he wasn't Dominic. Dominic was racked with guilt; he had committed the ultimate sin, according to his faith. To Dominic he had only fallen in love. He loved his church and he loved Theresa. "Why have I sinned?" he asked the Lord in his daily prayers.

One evening Jim returned from work and said there was an opportunity for promotion. It would mean they would have to move about 70 miles away and Jim thought that would be too far for him to commute on a daily basis. To Jim's surprise, Theresa agreed almost immediately.

She asked Jim not to tell anyone, especially their friends at the church. She said she didn't want a fuss. "We will tell them Jim, but only at the last minute." Jim went along with her wishes, as that's what he always did.

Jim had temporary accommodation with his new job until they sold their house. There was no need for a 'For Sale' sign; they just left it in the hands of the estate agent.

A few days before Jim and Theresa were due to move, Theresa went to see Dominic.

"Dominic, I have some news for you and I don't think you are going to like it."

Dominic was distraught. "Theresa, I can't lose you. I can't."

"I know Dominic, my heart is breaking too, but if things continue you will resent me for the consequences that will happen."

They made love one more time and cried together.

Jim and Theresa moved and within a few months Theresa discovered she was pregnant. Seven months later a little girl was born whom they named Isabelle. When Isabelle was five years old and Anthony was ten, Jim sadly passed away. Theresa was upset, of course she was, but she always held Dominic in her heart.

Eventually her children went off to university and started to lead their own lives. Isabelle was the first child to announce she was getting married. She had known Tom for four years; in fact, they met at university. Tom was also a Catholic and he and Isabelle had decided to get married in the Catholic Church in Tom's town. There were two reasons for this. Firstly, Tom's mum was in a wheelchair and it would make life a lot easier for her if she didn't have to travel far. Secondly, Tom loved the church where he had been christened and when he showed it to Isabelle, she loved it too.

Isabelle looked beautiful in her ivory satin and lace gown. Theresa wished Jim could see her, but was so proud of Anthony as he walked his sister down the aisle. Tom and Isabelle stood at the altar. They were getting married at the church of The Sacred Heart, where Theresa had met Father Brown all those years ago. Her heart filled with love as she wondered where he was now.

The priest came forward to welcome the congregation to be part of Tom and Isabelle's special day. He had the most wonderful silver-grey hair and a voice like velvet. *That voice!* she thought. *It can't be.* She looked more closely. Yes, they were all there: the beautiful brown eyes, the soft voice and the smile that had melted her heart all those years ago. All the ingredients to make Father Dominic Brown. "Oh my God, this is incredible," she whispered.

The service was so beautiful and Father Brown had given a lovely reading about love and relationships, leaving a lot of the guests in tears. You would have thought he was in love himself. Theresa realised he was doing what he was meant to be doing. She decided to avoid contact with Dominic, but only because she loved him. They couldn't have both lives and she knew it. She was so pleased to have seen him doing what he was called to do.

Tom and Isabelle were so moved by Father Brown's reading that they called at his house to thank him before they set off on their honeymoon.

Father Brown placed his hand gently on Isabelle's head and said, "Bless you my child."

Isabelle looked at him and replied, "Thank you Father."

Little did they know that no truer words had ever been spoken.

15

My Easter Angel

Sunday Mass was over and the church car park at St. Peter's flooded with parishioners exchanging news of the past week's events. A purple coat stood out from the middle of the gathering; it was the coat of Nancy Kelly. Nancy was a single parent to her daughter Sinead and her background was an Irish Catholic family. Nancy's faith meant a lot to her and she was gently guiding her daughter in the same direction.

Each Sunday after Mass, Nancy and Sinead would call round to Sinead's granny, as she was not able to go to Mass any more.

Sinead loved her granny and she liked to read St. Peter's newsletter to her each week. Granny loved to be informed of the happenings at the church.

"Oh, listen to this one Granny, they are organising a trip to Rome to see the Pope give his Easter blessing. Oh Granny, I would just love to go and see that."

As Nancy was making the coffee she overheard the conversation and felt quite surprised that Sinead had expressed such an interest. *In your dreams*, she thought. *There is no way we could afford that.*

When Nancy returned home Sinead's conversation with Granny regarding the trip to Rome was niggling away in her mind. She knew she couldn't possibly afford it, but would dearly love to make Sinead's dream come true. Not only was it Sinead's dream, but Nancy had always wanted to visit the Vatican, the heart of her faith. *One day maybe, one day,* she thought.

Next day, after Nancy finished her morning shift at the supermarket, she made a visit to the library. She loved to read, though buying books was not in her budget.

It was a chilly afternoon, as spring was still disguising herself as winter. Nancy arrived home with her bundle of books, lit her fire and, although feeling guilty, decided to settle down with a cup of tea and indulge in a blissful afternoon of reading. As she opened her book, an envelope fell out onto the floor. There was a name and address, which read:

Arthur Tutbury, 31 Rising Lane. Oh bless, she thought, *it must have been his bookmark*. Then she noticed that a little piece of pink paper had slipped out of the envelope when it fell to the floor. On picking it up, she could see more clearly that it was a lottery ticket. She looked at the date and it was two weeks old. Immediately she thought that it must be a 'dud', but she would check it out just in case. She popped the ticket back in the envelope and left it in the book.

By the end of the week, Nancy had finished her book. She had been so engrossed with her reading and having to change shifts at work that she had completely forgotten about the lottery ticket.

"I suppose I had better check it," she said to herself.

Reaching for her TV remote she brought up Teletext. Scrolling down, she found the date that was on the ticket. She called each number out loud as she went across the line. Not a single match did she find.

"Well, there's a surprise," she muttered and placed the ticket on the coffee table.

Nancy walked into the kitchen to prepare the evening meal, as Sinead would be home soon.

"Hello Mum. I'm home," Sinead called out, as she came through the door.

"Hello sweetheart, dinner won't be long."

Sinead went into the living room to watch her favourite soap.

"Have you been buying a lottery ticket Mum?" she shouted out.

"Don't worry," came the reply, "it's a dud,"

Sinead walked into the kitchen.

"Hope you remembered to check the raffle number as well."

"Yes, yes," replied Nancy. "Come on now, your dinner is ready."

Later on in the evening, after Sinead had gone to bed, her words about the raffle number were ringing in Nancy's head.

What did she mean raffle number? It's a lottery ticket.

She picked up the ticket which was still lying on the coffee table. As she scrutinised the ticket she saw what Sinead had meant.

"Oh dear," she sighed, "I had better check it I suppose."

She really wanted another read before bedtime, rather than to go through the tedious motions of finding Teletext. She drew the lottery ticket closer.

"Right, I am looking for a line starting with Jade. Oh there are a few of those," she said to herself.

As her eyes continued to scroll down the columns, they stopped abruptly. "No, that can't be right," she said. She checked it again and again, and again, and again. "Oh my God! Oh my God! Oh my God, I have a winning ticket!"

Now her dilemma had begun. Should she return the ticket to Mr. Tutbury, or should she cash it in? After all, there was no name on the ticket. She decided to sleep on it. Needless to say, her sleep was pretty disturbed that night.

It was Sunday morning and Nancy woke feeling riddled with guilt at even contemplating keeping the winning ticket when she knew exactly where the owner lived. She made a promise to herself that she would return it after Sinead had gone to school on Monday morning. Mr. Tutbury's home was only walking distance away.

Nancy and Sinead attended Sunday Mass as usual, but today was a little different, as Nancy still felt laden down with guilt over the lottery ticket. She lit candles and repented repeatedly.

It was now Monday morning and Sinead had left for school. Nancy carefully took the envelope, complete with lottery ticket, out of her book and placed it carefully into her handbag. She put on her purple coat and set out on the fifteen minutes' walk to Mr. Tutbury's house in Rising Lane.

She nervously rang the doorbell. It took a while for him to answer, as he was a bit stiff in the joints. He wasn't used to visitors, so was a little surprised to see Nancy standing there. Nancy started to explain about the library book, but as Mr. Tutbury couldn't stand for long, he asked her to come inside. She eventually got to the end of the saga and Mr. Tutbury looked into her eyes and smiled kindly.

"Do you know my dear, your honesty has restored my faith in human kindness. You are a good woman. I am an old man and I do not need that lottery ticket. Would you please accept it from me? I only buy one occasionally for something to do. I never expect to win. I don't need to win. I have no family and it would give me great pleasure for you to keep it."

Nancy was stunned. She insisted she couldn't keep it.

"If you could have one wish what would it be?" he asked.

Nancy told him about the trip to Rome at Easter to see the delivery of the Pope's blessing.

"Well, what are you waiting for?" He chuckled. "Didn't you know that God moves in mysterious ways? And when you are there, light a candle for me."

"Mr. Tutbury, you are my Easter Angel. That's what you are, my Easter Angel."

16

The Bracelet

Helen Hall and Ruth Carter had both been placed in the foster care of Mr. and Mrs Wood when they were 12 years old. Helen's father was a heroin addict who sadly lost his life to his controlling monster. This made Helen's mother up her intake of alcohol on a daily basis. So much so that it was impossible for her to care for Helen. Ruth was the child of a single mother with a severe mental illness. Each time her mother was sectioned Ruth was looked after by her Grandma, until the older woman's health deteriorated and she was placed in a care home.

The girls could empathise with each other and became the best of friends while in foster care. Helen and Ruth had found peace and happiness at last.

Mr. and Mrs. Wood were a delightful couple who cared for their foster children with a firm hand and a warm heart. Helen and Ruth were flourishing under the care, love and comfort that Mr. and

Mrs. Wood provided. Their warm clean beds, a home-cooked family meal and a hearty, healthy breakfast all had a huge impact on their school work. They were alert, interested and becoming enthusiastic about their grades.

Helen decided she wanted to become a teacher. There was a time in her life when that would not have been in her wildest dreams. Although Ruth was enjoying school, she had no idea what she wanted to be or do when she left school.

It was a wet Saturday afternoon in the school holidays. Helen and Ruth were at a loss as to how to spend their time. Homework was up to date, bedrooms had been cleaned and the luncheon dishes were washed and put away. Mrs. Wood perceived the girls were restless and needed a bit of inspiration to lift them out of their lethargy.

"Now then girls. I have just the thing for you to occupy yourselves. Just wait here and I'll be back in five minutes."

Helen and Ruth were intrigued. They giggled as Mrs. Wood made her way upstairs. Before long, they could hear thuds and thumps coming from the bottom of the wardrobe in the room up above. Five minutes later, Mrs. Wood appeared sounding rather breathless and carrying a large wooden box. With a heavy sigh she unloaded it onto the dining room table.

"Now girls, I have never told you about my love for beads. In this box you will find little bags of every sort of gem stone you could imagine. I think it would be nice to make yourselves a bracelet. I can start you off. It would be a sort of memento to carry with you when you go out into the big wide world."

She took the lid off the box. The girls stood with their mouths wide open.

"Wow! Where did you get all these beautiful beads?" asked Helen.

"Well, my father's work took him to the Far East and he always brought me some beads back. I have made lots of jewellery with them over the years. So have a good look and choose some for yourselves."

The choice of beads was tremendous and eventually the girls chose lapis and silver beads and decided to make two identical bracelets. They placed a silver heart-shaped bead in the centre of their bracelet and agreed there wouldn't be another bracelet in the world the same as theirs. The girls declared they would wear their bracelets forever.

Helen and Ruth were eternally grateful that they had been placed in the care of Mr. and Mrs. Wood. They each felt they had gained a sister and continued to feel safe and loved.

Their school days were coming to an end and Helen had obtained the grades she needed to be accepted at university. Ruth had no desire to go to university, but was successful at her interview with a local department store. She loved contact with people and couldn't wait to start her first job.

Helen would be moving 200 miles away. Mr. and Mrs. Wood had spent their lifetime saying sad farewells to their foster children, but saying goodbye to Helen and Ruth had an extra sadness as their two girls, who had become sisters, were parting too.

In the weeks and months that followed, Helen and Ruth stayed in touch, but as the years went by and Helen had graduated and qualified as a teacher, their communication became less and less until it eventually stopped.

Fourteen years had elapsed since Helen started teaching English to 11 and 12 year olds. One day while she was in the staff room, she picked up the Guardian newspaper and noticed a vacancy at her old school, in the town where she was fostered. She was ready for a change, so decided to apply. Four months later, Helen was back in her old town, living a couple of streets away from her foster home.

Mr. and Mrs. Wood had retired to the coast some years ago. Helen went to the department store where Ruth had gone to work. She looked in every department, but there was no sign of Ruth and none of the other assistants knew of her.

Helen was starting her new school on Monday morning. Oh how those memories came flooding back. The Headmistress showed Helen the way to her classroom and introduced her to her form. The children seemed very accepting of Miss Hall and were very attentive and polite. As the bell rang for break the children filed out of class chatting, giggling and probably exchanging comments about their new teacher. There was one pupil who was still struggling to put away her books and pack her satchel. Helen went over and knelt down beside her.

"Hello, can I help you sort your satchel?"

The young girl smiled. "I'm just looking for my bracelet."

"Your bracelet?"

"Yes, we can't wear jewellery in school, so I carry my bracelet with me."

She sighed a sigh of relief and produced the bracelet from a little cloth pouch at the bottom of her satchel. Helen asked if she could see it. As the bracelet emerged from the pouch Helen couldn't believe her eyes. It was the bracelet that she had made with Ruth on that wet Saturday afternoon at Mrs. Wood's.

"Oh that's beautiful. Where did you get it?"

"I'm adopted. I was told my mother left it for me when I was born."

Helen looked at this little figure with such sad eyes.

"Well I am so glad you have found your bracelet. Make sure you always keep it safe; it looks very special to me. I'm sorry, what is your name?"

The little girl looked at Miss Hall lovingly and replied,

"I'm Helen. My name is Helen."

17

The Car Keys

Snow had fallen during the night, creating a silence over the earth. Lights, kettles and coffee percolators were being switched on around the village and very soon that virgin snow that had formed so perfectly will be destroyed by car tyres, footprints and stains of yellow from exercised dogs. Nature's work of art will be defaced before it has had time to be admired. Such are the consequences of busy lives.

One of the busy lives in the village is that of Stella Hopkins. Stella is single and some may think she has all the time in the world; how wrong could they be. Three doors down from Stella, behind the faded curtains of number 16, lives Alice Hopkins, Stella's mother. Alice has always enjoyed ill health, but in reality it is her excuse to lean on Stella. She is only in her early sixties, quite attractive and looks as fit as a fiddle. Her expectations of her daughter are totally unreasonable and Stella feels obliged to succumb to her mother's demands. In her heart of hearts she knows her mother is exaggerating her ailments – that's if they even exist – in order to keep her close by. Alice didn't feel any guilt controlling her daughter's life.

It was hard for Stella to form any sort of lasting relationship. For one thing, there wasn't the opportunity for her to meet new people. Stella always returned home after work to cook her mother's meal and weekends were taken up with her mother's shopping and cleaning, not to mention the washing and ironing. Stella had brought home a couple of boyfriends she had met at work, but when she introduced them to her mother, Alice was so unfriendly towards them that she made life impossible for Stella and it wasn't much fun for the boyfriends.

Stella would love to move away; she feels like she is in chains. Her responsibility towards her mother is so great that she would never forgive herself if anything did happen to Alice. Her mother's behaviour was nothing more than emotional blackmail.

Some of the footprints in that early morning virgin snow belonged to Stella. Her early morning walks are her little bit of freedom. Her freedom to think and get away from demanding phone calls. Every now and then she would slide in the snow as she did as a child. Her red woolly hat covered her ears, you could see her hot breath as it hit the cold air. As she had one last slide she lost her balance. As she hit the ground her hand pushed into the snow unearthing what looked like car keys.

"My word," she said out loud. "What do I do with these?"

Stella returned home, quickly showered and made her ritual visit to see her mother before driving to work.

On her return home in the evening she called at the village shop to put a note in their window, saying that she had found car keys and details of her mobile number. Stella decided to carry the keys in her handbag in case she got a phone call. At least she would have them on her.

Months went by and no-one had called Stella enquiring about their car keys. In fact, she had almost forgotten about them herself. Alice knew nothing about Stella's fall and the keys. She would only give Stella advice she didn't need. It wasn't because she wanted to help; it was because she wanted to control everything in Stella's life.

Another Saturday morning had come around again, which meant a morning at the supermarket for Stella. This particular Saturday her shopping list wasn't very long and, as it was raining, she decided to use a basket instead of a trolley. That way she wouldn't have to return the trolley in the rain. She did, however, buy a little more than her list dictated. Her extra carrier bags made it hard for her to retrieve her keys from her handbag, but after a struggle trying to keep her bag on her shoulder and delving into her Tardis of a handbag, she managed to locate them under her glasses case. She awkwardly pressed her key fob to open the door.

Thank goodness for that, she thought. *I can't wait to drop this shopping.*

Stella dropped her bags on the back seat and quickly opened the driver's door as the rain was a little heavier now. Suddenly, out of the blue, someone shouted: "Excuse me, what are you doing?"

Stella looked up puzzled. A very smart gentleman stood before her. He had piercing blue eyes, as blue as the sky on a summer's day.

"What do you mean what am I doing?"

"Well this is my car!" he exclaimed.

"I am really sorry, but this is my car."

The stranger was getting worried now. Who was this person he was encountering? He was trying to think quickly before she drove away.

"What is your number plate?" he asked.

Stella was now assuming that this man must be a real weirdo and she too had to think quickly.

Right, she thought. *I will tell him and with a bit of luck, he will go away.* She recited her registration number to him.

He laughed sarcastically and said, "Well that's not the registration of the car you are sitting in."

"What, are you mad?" she cried.

"Get out and have a look if you don't believe me. Look, your car is next to mine."

Stella huffed and puffed and resentfully got out of her car to look. Sure enough, he was right. Her car was the same colour and model and it was parked next to his.

"Oh my God, I am so sorry."

He looked at her with a wry smile on his face. "What I would like to know is, how on earth did you get in my car with your keys?"

Stella glared back at him and stuttered. "I-I don't know. It's a mystery to me too.

A light came on in her mind. "Of course, of course. I do know how I did it now."

"Well would you mind sharing it with me, as it is a complete mystery to me?" he said with exhaustion.

Stella told him the whole story of how she had found the keys buried in the snow and it was so long ago that she had forgotten they were still in her handbag. Fortunately, they both saw the funny side and laughed out loud.

"I'm sorry, my name is Peter. I should be thanking you for keeping my keys safe. I do remember quite a few months ago I did lose my keys. I ran out of petrol and had to abandon my car 'til morning and walked home. It snowed during the night so there was no chance of me finding them. Good job I had a spare key."

"Well," said Stella, "all's well that ends well."

"Look," Peter said, "can I buy you a coffee? It is the least I can do to repay you for your kindness. Lots of folk would have thrown the keys away."

Stella's thoughts went into overdrive. *What about Mother? I did prepare her sandwiches for lunch and she is quite capable of making a cup of tea. It would be so nice to converse with someone new.*

Her mind was racing.

"Ok," she replied, "that would be nice. I can't stay long though, as I have to get back for mother."

After settling in at the supermarket café, Peter asked Stella if her mother was ill.

"That's a good question," Stella replied.

One hour later and Stella couldn't believe she had opened her heart to a complete stranger. Peter seemed very kind and he had listened attentively and with understanding. During their conversation it transpired that Peter and Stella's mother both had a love of roses.

Stella checked her watch. "My goodness, I must fly. Mother will be wondering what has happened to me." She turned and held out her hand to Peter. "It was nice to meet you."

"Likewise," said Peter. "I-I was thinking," Peter said clumsily, "as your mother has a love of roses, would you like to bring her to see my garden. The roses are looking quite spectacular at the moment."

Stella looked shocked. "That is a lovely thought Peter, but my mother is becoming a bit of a hermit, yet it would be so good for her to get out."

"Look, this is my phone number. You can only but ask. I live on my own and it would be nice for me to show off my roses, especially to someone who appreciates them."

"You are too kind. I must dash, but I will ring and let you know about Mother. Bye." Her voice faded into the distance.

As she drove back to see her mother Stella reflected on the encounter she had had with Peter. She really couldn't believe she had just literally met a stranger and told him about her dilemma with Mother. Stella decided not to mention Peter and his roses today; she would wait until Sunday. She knew she was going to face the third degree from Alice as she had taken so long over the shopping.

After their meal on Saturday evening Stella told her mother she was going home early as she was tired and wanted an early night. "I will be round in the morning Mum. I have bought a chicken for lunch."

As promised, faithful Stella arrived at her mother's house three doors down with all the ingredients to make a tasty Sunday lunch. She was going over the conversation in her mind as to how to tell her mother about Peter and the invitation to visit his garden. And she knew she was going to have to lie a little.

After lunch Stella made a cup of tea and bravely broached the subject of Peter.

"Mum, you know how you love your roses, well a friend of mine has very kindly invited us to visit his garden as he has some spectacular roses."

"What, is that a friend from work?" snapped Alice.

"No Mum, not from work. It's just someone I have got to know from the supermarket."

"Supermarket? Do you always meet men at the supermarket?"

"I haven't met him in that sense; it's someone I talk to from time to time. For goodness sake, I am allowed to talk to people. I just thought it would be nice for you to go out and look at something you love."

"I'll think about it," Alice replied in a dogmatic manner. Her response told Stella not to mention it again – for a while anyway.

A week passed by and neither Stella nor Alice had mentioned Peter and his rose garden. Stella was losing patience with her mother and thought she really didn't deserve to be treated kindly.

Another Sunday, another lunch and Stella decided she would broach the subject again. With lunch eaten and washing up done, Stella was just about to mention Peter, when out of character Alice piped up, "Well when are we going to visit this rose garden? The summer will have gone if we don't go soon."

The next day, Stella phoned Peter, hoping he was true to his word and still welcomed a visit from

Stella and Alice. Peter was delighted and they arranged a visit for the following Saturday afternoon.

Stella picked Alice up at one o'clock as arranged. Peter lived at the other end of the village so it would only take minutes to get there. Alice looked somewhat drab wearing her ancient navy anorak.

"Why don't you put your nice green coat on Mum?" suggested Stella.

"Oh no, I keep that for best."

"But Mum, you don't go anywhere."

"This will do me fine. I'm only looking round a garden."

Stella raised her eyebrows in frustration and decided not to push it. Alice being Alice could call the whole thing off.

Peter's driveway was quite long and had plenty of room for parking. He had seen them arriving and opened the door to greet them. Stella had given Peter the low down on what she had told Alice about how they'd met, so he was fully briefed.

"Hello, welcome, you must be Alice."

"How'd you do," Alice replied curtly. She had lost the art of socialising; her social skills were virtually non-existent.

Peter smiled. "I understand you love roses?" He gave a little wink to Stella. "Shall we have a look in the garden first? Then we can come in and have a nice cup of tea."

The more they walked round the garden, which wasn't small, the more relaxed Alice became. Peter was so easy to talk to and could answer all Alice's questions about roses. She was impressed. But, of course, she never let it show.

As Peter's beautiful hallway clock chimed four o'clock, Stella thought it was time they made a move. Alice had always told her never to outstay her welcome.

"Well" Peter said, "it has been so nice to have your company. Now you know where I am you could always take a walk down to see me when Stella is at work. Don't be a stranger."

Alice looked back at Peter in surprise. "What with my hips?" she exclaimed.

"Nonsense, a bit of exercise will do you the power of good."

Alice had never been dismissed like that before and it left her quite speechless.

They arrived back at Alice's house at about 4.15pm. "You know Mum, it really isn't far to Peter's. It would be nice for you and him if you visited from time to time as you do have a common interest." Stella prepared tea and sandwiches, but Alice didn't mention her day.

A few weeks later Stella received a phone call from Peter.

"Hello Stella, how are you?"

"Fine, thank you Peter. Nice to hear from you."

"Stella, I was wondering, I am going to visit a rose grower as I am a member of the village Garden Centre's gardening club. I thought Alice might like to accompany me. What do you think?"

"Oh Peter, that sounds lovely and so kind of you to think of her. I will ask Mother this evening and let you know." Stella didn't think for one moment that Alice would go, but surprisingly she said she would.

The following Sunday Stella called in on Alice to take her to Peter's. Alice was ready and waiting in her best green coat, pearl earrings and a touch of lipstick. Stella was gobsmacked. *Is that really Mother?* she thought.

"Mum you look lovely."

"It's only my green coat, nothing special."

Alice found it hard to give compliments and even harder to receive them. If anyone could bring

Alice out of herself, crack open the shell she had cocooned herself in, it was Peter. He was a gentleman; he made her laugh, made her feel special and made her happy. He had changed her life.

They had several more outings and even started to go to a tea dance on Tuesday afternoons. Stella was amazed at her mother's transformation, as not only did Peter change Alice's life, but he had changed Stella's life too. He had given her back her freedom.

18

The Coat

It was almost two years since Robert Goddard's twin sister Sheila had died in a tragic car accident on a beautiful sunny autumn afternoon. Robert was heartbroken and too grief-stricken to sort through Sheila's belongings, they were still as she had left them in her London flat. Losing Sheila made him feel like he'd had a limb amputated.

Robert lived in a little stone cottage in the north east of the country. He used to go and visit Sheila once a month and they would speak on the telephone almost daily. They were both fortunate enough to own their own properties. Paradoxically, the circumstances that had given them that good fortune was the death of their parents, who had also died in a tragic car crash. Their inheritance had given the twins the opportunity to be mortgage-free.

Sheila was single and had left everything to Robert in her Will. He knew the time had come to put her flat on the market and finalise her estate. The thing he was dreading most was packing Sheila's clothes into charity bags. Bricks and mortar are just bricks and mortar, but Sheila's clothes were Sheila. Every crease at the elbows, every bow that was tied, every button undone, had been done by her. Her perfume escaped into the room when the wardrobe door was opened.

Robert extended his statutory Easter leave and made the car journey down to London on Maundy Thursday. On arriving at the flat, he was saddened by the sight of two pots of cheerful daffodils that Sheila had planted soon after she had moved in. She loved the freshness, new growth and hope that spring symbolised for her.

Robert decided he would have a takeaway that evening and start the daunting task of 'clearing' after a good night's sleep.

Two days passed and Robert had certainly broken the back of sorting through Sheila's belongings, categorising them into different groups of rubbish, keep and charity. He had decided to keep the jewellery as he hoped he might have a daughter of his own one day and it would be nice to pass some items on to her.

Robert looked through numerous photo albums and talked to Sheila as he did so. Each photo triggered a memory, especially the ones of their childhood days. It had been a hugely emotional task for him. His eyes were red and swollen from releasing tears and feelings that had been locked inside for the past two years.

After arranging the sale of the flat with the estate agent, he disposed of the rubbish bags, arranged for a charity to pick up the furniture and piled bags of Sheila's clothes into his car to take to the charity shop. There would be some beautiful finds for some lucky customers. Sheila had always liked to buy quality rather than quantity. He would drop the clothes off before his long journey home.

As he got into his car, he glanced back at the flat. He saw the daffodils gently swaying in the breeze and no longer felt saddened. He couldn't leave them. He promptly got out of his car and placed the pots in his boot. In that moment, he knew he would put Sheila's daffodils outside the front door of his little stone cottage. He felt that each spring she would be making an appearance to him – a thought which he found quite comforting.

Life was returning to normal for Robert. Sheila's daffodils were in pride of place and looked so pretty either side of his stable door.

The shock of Sheila's death and the heavy burden of responsibility to finalise her affairs was slowly starting to lessen. He had been in a very dark place, losing all motivation and his love of socialising.

Twelve months had passed, and Sheila's daffodils were flowering like they had never flowered before. They brought a warm and loving smile to Robert's face every time he walked out of his cottage. He wasn't an overly religious man, but he had been raised a Catholic and as Easter was approaching, he had a deep longing to attend Mass. He Googled the Mass times at his local parish and decided he would go to the 8pm Easter Mass on the Saturday night.

He was feeling quite nervous as he pulled into the church car park. Several years had passed since Robert had attended Mass. He had fallen out with God when his parents had both been killed in that awful car crash.

I hope I remember what to do, he thought, as he dipped his fingers into the holy water font and blessed himself.

He wanted to stay as inconspicuous as he could, so he went upstairs to the balcony. He was almost feeling not worthy enough to be there. He was having a Catholic guilt moment for staying away so long. He genuflected, knelt at the end of the pew and said an Act of Contrition before Mass started.

The church looked beautiful and there was a wonderful aroma of fresh flowers. It was lit by candlelight and each parishioner held a lighted candle. Robert didn't have a candle; he had forgotten to pick one up at the door. He felt like a fish out of water.

Suddenly there was a gentle tap on his shoulder. He turned. A young woman with shoulder length hair and a warm smile handed him a lit candle.

"Oh, thank you."

Her act of kindness made him feel welcome. He actually felt he belonged.

There were stairs to the side which led down into the main congregation. The young woman proceeded to walk down the stairs, Robert watched her as she went. He turned to look back at the altar and then realised what he had just seen.

The young woman was wearing a coat. A coat that Robert had only ever seen once before. And that coat had belonged to Sheila. She had it tailor-made when she visited Hong Kong. She'd chosen the beautiful brocade ivory fabric and had it lined with a gorgeous navy lining. The pocket tops and collar edging were trimmed with navy to match the lining. Robert smiled, as he remembered Sheila telling him that the tailor subtly embroidered the initials of his customers on their garments. He had put Sheila's initials on the cuff of the sleeve.

His mind had completely wandered off the Mass. How could a coat that was bespoke for Sheila in

Hong Kong and put in a charity shop in London end up in a little town in Northumberland?

His thoughts were taking over, but were abruptly interrupted as the young woman returned to the balcony. She held out a collection box in front of Robert. He fumbled for his wallet and managed to pull out a five-pound note. As he placed it in the box, he managed to see the initials on the sleeve of the coat. S.G. Sheila Goddard.

It must be Sheila's coat, it must be, he thought.

Before he knew it, the young woman had turned away and was collecting money elsewhere.

Mass was over and Robert slipped away quietly down the back stairs, through the church porch and into the car park. As he reached his car, he heard a voice call, "Excuse me." It was the young woman with the warm smile who had given him the lighted candle.

"You left your scarf. I always check the pews for left items."

"Oh, thank you so much and thank you again for my candle."

"That's ok, it's what I do. Are you new to the parish? I haven't seen you before."

Robert thought she was very attractive and there was definitely a connection between them.

"I have been in the parish a few years now, but I'm afraid I have been a bit of a lapsed Catholic," he admitted.

"Don't worry, it happens. Maybe see you next week."

Robert's thoughts were hurtling through his mind. *Should I ask her about the coat? No, I'll wait till next week.* "Yes, see you next week," he replied. "Sorry, what's your name?"

"Oh, I'm Sally, Sally Graham. Got to go. Bye."

Sally Graham, he thought. *SG – Sally Graham.*

The following week seemed long as Robert couldn't wait to attend Saturday night Mass again. It wasn't as much for the Mass; it was because he wanted to meet with Sally again. He did receive some good news from his solicitor that week and that was to say that after some problems, contracts had been signed and finally Sheila's flat had been sold.

Saturday evening Mass had finally arrived and Robert felt both nervous and excited. He took a seat in the balcony as he had done the previous week. His eyes scanned the congregation below looking for Sally. He was hoping she would be wearing the coat. If he got the opportunity, he might pluck up the courage to ask her where she had got it. It was difficult to recognise people and all Robert could see was a sea of heads.

It was that time in the Mass when the collection box came round. Robert looked towards the stairs. He heard tiny footsteps on the wooden treads. Sure enough, Sally appeared like a vision of loveliness, but she was not wearing the beautiful ivory coat. As she held the box in front of Robert they exchanged smiles and whispered, "Hello."

After Mass Sally went to find Robert and invited him to join some of the parishioners in the hall for coffee. It wouldn't be Robert's first choice to be spending Saturday evening in the church hall drinking coffee, but he accepted without a second thought. They chatted away very easily and Sally introduced him to several members of the choir and the parish priest, Father John. Robert didn't feel at ease talking to the priest, probably because he had been away from the church for some time.

The shutter of the serving hatch into the kitchen started to rattle as it was lowered quite abruptly. Coffee cups were being cleared away and echoes of "Night". Night" could be heard fading into the night air.

"Well, it looks like it is throwing-out time," Robert joked.

"Look, are you free for dinner one evening?"

Blimey, he thought, *did I just say that?*

Sally blushed slightly. "Oh that would be lovely, thank you."

They swapped phone numbers and walked out to the car park.

"I will call you tomorrow Sally."

"Thank you Robert. I will look forward to that."

Robert drove home singing at the top of his voice, feeling happier than he had in a long time. He was sure Sheila was looking after him.

Robert called Sally as promised and they arranged to meet on Wednesday evening. On his way over to meet her, he was hoping she would be wearing the lovely ivory coat. He arrived at her house dead on the dot of seven o'clock. Sally was ready and waiting. As her front door opened, Robert's eyes lit up. She was wearing the coat.

He got out of the car to greet her. "You look beautiful. Your coat is stunning."

"Thank you Robert. You are looking very smart yourself."

When they were settled in the restaurant Robert plucked up the courage to ask about her coat.

"Sally, your coat is so unusual. You must have bought it somewhere special?"

"Actually Robert, you would never guess, but I bought it from a charity shop in London. When I saw the initials SG on the cuff, that clinched it; I thought it was definitely for me."

Robert quietly gathered his composure.

"Hmm, do you go to London often?"

"Only since my brother moved down there last year. In fact, two weeks ago he signed the contract on a flat."

19

The Dressing Table

I woke this morning feeling excited and yet with some trepidation. I stare at the ceiling; it is the same ceiling I have woken up to since I was a child, except this morning I am looking at it with much more awareness.

The tiny hairline cracks that have lived in the coving all these years become more noticeable. Further down the wall is a redundant hook that has never held a picture, but has been painted over several times. My eyes move across to my curtains that have dutifully shaded me from the light. They are pretty curtains, but look even prettier today.

My tummy has butterflies. My excitement returns. Today I am leaving my parents' house, my shelter since childhood, to move into my very own flat. My trepidation comes from knowing that every bill that comes through my letterbox will be my responsibility for payment. In my mind, I quickly change the word responsibility for privilege. I am a big believer that the words we use are catalysts to how we feel. I do have an income, therefore I can pay a bill, so I regard that as a privilege. Positivity rules OK for me.

I have concluded my goodbyes to my bedroom with overwhelming fondness and gratitude.

The estate agents are expecting me to collect my keys at 11am. It is so important to do this, as I am taking delivery of my new bed at 11.30am. My trusted friends have formed a little army and are going into action to collect and deliver my belongings in the afternoon. I have managed to negotiate a good deal on the white goods in the kitchen at the flat. Mum and Dad have been so kind and along with several pieces of furniture they have given me, they have also bought me a sofa. The only thing I need is a dressing table.

My flat is one of four in a converted large Victorian house – my favourite style of architecture. Although it saddens me that the house has had some of its originality stolen by the conversion, the thought of living in a modern flat would make my skin crawl.

It is nearly midnight; I am sitting in darkness, with the generosity of the outside street lamp sharing its light. I reflect on the day's happenings. I thank God for my parents' generosity and the helping hands of my friends. Tomorrow is a new day; tomorrow I will wake to a different ceiling.

I haven't moved too far from my parents' home and I now actually live closer to my granddad who I absolutely adore. He is over the moon that I will be able to pop in for a cup of tea more often than I have previously.

As I wearily climb into my new bed, I make a promise to myself to go and see Granddad tomorrow.

Granddad lives in a little maisonette, which is ideal for him – not too big and not too small. It is a ground-floor maisonette which again is ideal as it means he can feed the birds. He would be lost without his little feathered friends. If he is not feeding them, he sits by the window and gets so much pleasure watching them flit from branch to branch.

Exhausted from yesterday's move, I wake a little later this morning. Church bells ring out in the distance as the sun streams through my window. "Oh it's good to be alive," I say to myself.

Throwing back the duvet, I shower quickly, have breakfast and head off to Granddad's. I can't wait to tell him about my new flat. He always takes an interest in everything I do.

On arriving at Granddad's, I find him sitting outside on his little bench with a mug of tea in his hand.

"Hello my dear," he says lovingly. "How lovely to see you and there's plenty more tea in the pot."

I kiss him gently on the forehead. "Hello Granddad, you stay there. I'll go and pour myself a cup."

I join him on his little bench and tell him all about my flat and how the move went yesterday.

"Now then," he says firmly, "what else do you need for this flat? I want to buy you something."

"Well Granddad, I do need a dressing table, but it won't cost a lot, as I am looking for an old second-hand one and I don't think they are fetching a lot of money these days."

"Why don't you look in my free paper? There is always furniture for sale and it will be local."

As usual, my granddad is right and there are pages of 'stuff' for sale. I find two dressing tables that sound interesting, so I will arrange to view them after work tomorrow.

"Thank you so much Granddad. If I buy one of the dressing tables, I will take you to the flat, then you can see what you have bought me and look round the flat at the same time."

Today seems to be passing so slowly as I am impatient to go and view my dressing tables.

When I eventually get to leave the office the traffic is against me; every traffic light changes to red on my approach.

The first house I arrive at is selling the most expensive dressing table. The house looks unloved with a crashed car on the lawn. I rap on the door knocker, which is holding on by a single nail and announce myself to the young woman who opens the door. Cigarette smoke greets me and hangs in the air like yesterday's washing. I am escorted in and then introduced to the advertised item. *What a pitiful over-priced piece of junk*, I think. I glance across at the young woman. She is looking at me optimistically.

"I am so sorry, it's not as old as I had imagined."

Her optimistic look changes in a flash, as smoke billows out of her nostrils.

"Well me mam bought it in the sixties. It is quite old," she says knowingly.

She is so misguided in thinking it is old or interesting enough to command the price she is asking. I leave politely and apologise for any inconvenience, although I am secretly thinking that the inconvenience is all mine.

As I start my ignition, I do wonder if it is worth my while to view the second dressing table. "I must go," I tell myself. "I am expected."

If kerb appeal can be relied upon, then this bungalow looks promising. The front lawn is neatly mowed and lobelia edging cascades over onto the crazy paving. I ring the door bell.

"Just a minute," I hear. Slowly the door opens to reveal a smartly dressed elderly lady.

"Sorry to keep you dear, but I had to put my cat in the front room. I worry about her getting on the road"

"That's alright," I reply. "I have come about the dressing table."

"Yes dear, do come in."

I am led down the hall into the spare bedroom. I can hardly believe my eyes. There, standing in all its glory, is the most stunning dressing table. It has truly been loved and cared for and probably waxed every week. It is so beautiful that I am speechless. I stare in silence, my mouth open wide.

The old lady looks at me and says, "Are you alright my dear? Don't you like it? I expect you young things want something more modern."

I smile at her. "No, I don't like it, I love it. It is perfect. I will buy it."

I tell her I have a friend with a van and we will pick it up tomorrow evening.

I am feeling so happy as I drive home. I will fetch Granddad on Saturday morning. I can't wait to show him my beautiful dressing table.

Saturday morning comes around and Granddad is expecting me. I quickly get ready. I am so excited to show him his gift to me.

"Come on Granddad, steady as you go up these steps."

With Granddad safely installed in my flat, I tell him to close his eyes as I guide him into the bedroom.

"Right Granddad, open your eyes."

"My word, you have done well."

"Yes, I have, haven't I? I haven't had time to wax it yet."

"Give me the polish and I'll do it for you."

"Are you sure, Grand-dad? Then I'll make us a cup of tea."

After washing up my breakfast dishes, I appear back in the bedroom carrying two mugs of tea.

Granddad is sitting ashen-faced on the chair. He turns to look at me.

"Did you know you have a secret drawer?" he says shakily.

"A secret drawer!" I exclaim. "How utterly, utterly wonderful." But Granddad, you look a little pale, do you feel alright?"

He hands me a bundle of letters. "These were in the drawer and I wrote them. I wrote them during the war. She was, at the time, the love of my life."

"What! Oh Granddad, are you sure?"

"Oh I'm sure alright."

I look at an envelope, the address reads: 59 Alexandra Road. That is the same address where I went to buy the dressing table. I slip a letter out of an envelope to look at the signature. There it is, *with much love Richard.* Richard is my Granddad's name.

We drink our tea and talk about the possibility that the old lady from whom I bought my dressing table is the same lady who Granddad wrote to all those years ago.

"Why don't you phone her Granddad? I never got her name, but I still have her number. You only have to ask. After all, you have been saying you would like a partner to take to your tea dances on Wednesday afternoons."

I ring the number and hand the phone to Granddad. He takes my hand and squeezes it tightly. He is obviously very nervous and excited. I am praying it will be her; this is the sort of stuff dreams are made of.

"Hello," a little voice echoes down the phone.

Granddad looks startled. He splutters and stammers somewhat.

"Oh hello," he says shakily. "I hope you don't mind me asking, but are you Jessica? Jessica Harrington that was?"

"Yes, I am Jessica and I am still Jessica Harrington. Who would like to know, please?"

"Jessica, this is Richard, Richard Brown. Do you remember me?"

"Remember you, I have never forgotten you."

"And I have never forgotten you," replies Granddad.

I leave the room and let them talk in private.

As I walk back down the hall to the living room the smell of wax polish has permeated the flat and instantly transports me back to Granny's house. I think it is from her that I get my love of antiques. She died seven years ago. I miss her so much and Granddad is so lonely without her.

Suddenly my bedroom door opens. I see Granddad walking in a daze towards me.

"Come and sit down Granddad. You have had a bit of a shock."

"You can say that again. I never thought I would see her again."

He explains how they were sweethearts, but lost touch during the war. He never got replies to his letters and thought she had lost interest in him, so thought it best not to contact her after the war. However, during his phone call to Jessica, he learned that she did reply.

"Do you know, she loved me so much she couldn't love anyone else and lived in hope that one day I would find her? Can you believe that?"

"Yes Granddad, I can believe that, because you are so lovely and thank you again for my beautiful dressing table."

"No, thank you dear, for finding Jessica."

20

The Glass Teddy Bear

Annie Brown opened her eyes to a vibrant orange sky that melted like liquid amber into the sea. She had moved to Cornwall 15 years before, to start a new life and open up a small bric-a-brac shop.

Although her shop was a success and in some respects made her happy, the heartache she had taken to Cornwall had never gone away.

She was artistic by nature. Her home was calming, yet colourful; crystals glinted in the sunlight, while wind chimes tinkled in the breeze and everywhere there were things of beauty. There was confirmation of her creativity by a large basket overflowing with knitting wool that occupied a corner of her living room. Colourful and beautiful stained-glass art that she had carefully made adorned the windows. Her stained-glass hobby is something she is very passionate about and yet paradoxically reminds her of the heartache that she would rather not have experienced.

It was 17 years previously when her son John's marriage ended. It was a bitter divorce and John's ex-wife was very punishing not only to John, but also to Annie.

John and his ex-wife Emma had one daughter, Laura, who Annie absolutely adored. Laura in turn adored her granny and loved to visit her house, showing a fascination for all the beautiful and colourful objects.

Annie had made Laura a bright yellow stained glass teddy bear, which Laura loved and wanted it to be hung in her bedroom window. She loved to watch the morning sun light up teddy and in her little mind tell herself that teddy had woken up. On a cloudy morning she would tell herself that teddy was still sleeping. She would give an account of teddy's sleeping habits to her parents over breakfast; he had become her little friend.

Laura was seven years old when her parents got divorced. John had tried to have an amicable separation, but Emma was so controlling and manipulative that she was determined to cut all communication with John's family, particularly Annie.

Emma moved hundreds of miles away with Laura and returned the glass teddy bear to Annie. She saw teddy as a link between Laura and Annie. Because of her jealous nature, she wanted to eradicate all memories that Laura had of Annie.

She told Laura the colour of teddy would not go in her new bedroom. Despite Laura being heartbroken, Emma insisted teddy should be returned.

When Annie heard the news she was devastated. She felt bereaved. She had never felt such emotional pain. *How could one person deliberately do this to another?* she thought. *And more importantly, how could a mother deprive her daughter of her granny?*

Annie held teddy close to her. He had become real. He was Laura's friend and she vowed she would always look after teddy and keep him safe. Teddy was the remaining link that Annie had with her grand-daughter.

Annie's health was now starting to deteriorate; her emotional hurt was so great it was taking its toll on her physical and mental state. She was desperate: she had to change her life, otherwise she felt she would die. That is the heartache that Annie had taken to Cornwall.

She felt she could cope if she put even more miles between herself and Laura. No-one in her Cornish village had to know she even had a grand-daughter. Annie could stop the pretence and could stop giving fictitious reasons why she didn't see her grand-daughter. To tell the truth was just too painful. This alone lifted some of her stress.

The orange sky that had glowed so brightly earlier, was now changing to a soft yellow and Annie knew it really was time to get her warm lazy body up to greet the day. She opened her little shop at 10am, so there was time to shower and have a leisurely breakfast.

Annie loved her shop; it really was a place she could escape to, to heal her broken heart. The old-fashioned bell rang as she pushed open the door. Sunlight flooded through the window. Rainbows, created by crystals, danced around the walls.

Annie called out, "Good morning, are you asleep or awake?" No-one else was in the shop, but there, in pride of place, teddy hung in the window. Laura's glass teddy bear was still being loved and cared for by her granny; teddy was safe. Annie's daily ritual of greeting teddy was like connecting with Laura. Her second ritual was to make a cup of coffee. She disappeared into the tiny kitchen which was cleverly hidden by the most beautiful gold and aubergine chenille curtain.

Annie hardly had time to take the lid off the coffee jar when the shop bell rang. *Goodness*, she thought, *that's an early bird. My coffee will have to wait.*

As Annie pulled back the curtain to return to the shop, she saw a lovely young woman dressed in a tapestry coat, with matching scarf and the most striking floppy hat.

"Good morning," Annie said cheerfully. "Can I help you?"

The young woman smiled. "How much is the glass teddy bear hanging in the window?"

Annie froze, and then swallowed hard. "Oh I am afraid he is priceless. He is not for sale."

The young woman stared back into Annie's eyes with sadness in her own.

"Oh that's a shame. Can I ask where you bought him?"

"I didn't buy him. I made him a long, long time ago for a very special little girl."

The young woman's eyes filled with tears, flashed back to Annie's and said, "Is he asleep or awake?"

Annie's heart wanted to explode. "Laura? Are you Laura?"

"Yes. Yes Granny, I really am."

Tears flowed in abundance as Laura and Annie hugged each other tightly. Annie's heartache was finally over. She could never in her wildest dreams have foreseen this day.

Laura explained to her granny that she was pursuing her career as an artist and thought Cornwall was an excellent place to do just that.

Once Laura had really settled into her new life, she was able to help out in her granny's shop a few days a week. As for teddy, he was back in his rightful place, hanging in Laura's bedroom window.

21

The Mirror

It was a rainy Saturday afternoon in Oxford. The gentle breeze carpeted the wet cobbles with pink cherry blossom. Grace Snowden was in her final year of a law degree. She loved to walk across the cobbles and sense the energies of great scholars that had gone before. Grace had remained single at university. Studying for a law degree was enough to focus on without the added pressure of romantic complications. She had many friends and loved to socialise with good company. She relished debate, yet languished in solitude. A favourite pastime was rummaging through second-hand shops looking for that one special piece that had been overlooked and under-priced.

Grace's parents were quite wealthy, to say the least and always made sure there were adequate funds in her bank account, not to mention the converted Victorian luxury apartment that they were in the process of buying for her in time for her graduation. Grace knew how privileged she was and never took any aspect of her life for granted. She believed in life after death, sensed the presence of spirit and often displayed psychic insight.

As it was a rainy afternoon and Grace wanted some respite from studying, she decided to take herself off to try and find that under-priced special piece of *objet d'art*. Grace's favourite shop was hidden away off the main street, down a little cobbled alleyway. Before entering the shop she opened and closed her umbrella several times to shake off the rain. She then placed it just inside the doorway to finish dripping onto the coconut doormat.

"Hello Mr. Turnbull, it's a bit wet today, isn't it?"

"You can say that again," he replied as he looked up from his newspaper, peering over the top of his glasses. "And it doesn't do much for my arthritis, I can tell you."

"Oh I'm sorry," Grace replied sympathetically. "I'll just mooch around and I'll give you a shout if I need any help."

"You carry on my dear."

Grace had been mooching for about 15 minutes when she spied what looked like the side of a rosewood frame that was sandwiched between other frames. As she was contemplating the logistics of taking a closer look, the door bell rang and a tall, attractive man was walking towards her. She didn't want to disturb Mr. Turnbull, as she knew he was in pain today. Grace smiled at the attractive stranger, acting out the damsel in distress. He picked up on her body language and quietly asked if she needed any help.

"Oh, would you mind? That would be so helpful," Grace replied coyly.

Why have female charm and not use it once in a while? she thought.

The stranger was very tall and it was easy for him to slide the rosewood frame out of the grips of the other frames that nestled high on the wide, warped shelf. As it was lifted down, Grace could see it was more than a frame. It was a beautiful Victorian swivel mirror, with a little drawer in the base.

"Oh my word, it's beautiful. Thank you so much for your help... err... err..."

"Phillip. My name is Phillip."

"Well thank you, Phillip. I really appreciate your help."

Grace picked up the mirror and carried it to Mr. Turnbull to enquire on the price. Grace found the price very acceptable and bought it with her new flat in mind.

The rain had abated, which pleased Grace, as she didn't have to struggle holding up her umbrella. Her rented flat wasn't too far away, but she was glad to relieve her aching arms. Grace placed her new purchase on top of the chest of drawers in her bedroom; they went so well together. She loved the mirror and wondered who had owned it before. She liked the feel of it and sensed it had lovely energies. She cleaned and waxed it and the rosewood positively glowed.

A few evenings later, as Grace entered her bedroom, she glanced in admiration at her mirror. To her amazement and very fleetingly, she saw the face of a woman with a very kind smile. Grace wasn't at all fearful as she had encountered spirit experiences before.

The woman became a regular visitor in the mirror. So much so that Grace greeted her with "Good morning" when she woke up and "Good night" on retiring.

Grace left university with a first-class honours degree under her belt. She secured a position with a local firm of solicitors and was ready to move into her new flat. Despite having the security of the bank of Mummy and Daddy, Grace had worked hard for what she had achieved and thanked God every day for her blessings.

She moved into her flat and before long it was looking stunning, mainly furnished with all her bargain second-hand pieces. The mysterious woman in the mirror still visited from time to time, but not quite as often.

It was a cold, dark night and Grace had had a very heavy and stressful day in court. All she wanted to do was to have a nice hot meal on a tray and curl up on the sofa to clear her mind. Suddenly the door bell rang.

"Oh no!" moaned Grace. "That's all I want."

Grace carefully opened her door, with the safety chain still secured. She was startled. "Goodness, it's Phillip, isn't it?"

"Yes, that's right. Aren't you the young woman I helped in the second-hand shop? I never did get your name."

"Grace. I'm Grace."

"Well I am sorry to bother you Grace, but I live across the landing and my electricity has gone off. I just wondered if yours has too?"

"No, mine is fine. Would you like a coffee or something?"

"That's very kind of you, but I think it best if I get my electric sorted."

"Well maybe another time. Good luck with the electric."

The next evening Grace thought it would be very neighbourly if she knocked on Phillip's door to make sure his electricity was working. She nervously approached his door and tapped on it tentatively. Phillip answered almost immediately and assured her everything was fine. This time, Phillip asked Grace in for coffee and she accepted.

"Your flat is lovely Phillip. I see you like old furnishings too."

"Oh absolutely, wouldn't have anything else."

There was a beautiful silver photo frame on the mantelpiece. Grace couldn't believe her eyes. It contained a photo of the woman who appeared in her mirror. Grace plucked up the courage to ask Phillip who she was.

"That's my mother. She sadly died in a horse-riding accident when I was in my early twenties."

"I am so sorry Phillip. I shouldn't have asked."

"No worries," replied Phillip. "I like to talk about her. I miss talking to her. Do you know, she always knew I found it difficult to ask girls out and she always used to say she would find me a girl even if it took until after she died. She would joke and say she would find me one and send her to me from the spirit world."

Grace looked at Phillip, smiled and thought, *One day I will tell you how she did it.*

Grace never saw the woman in the mirror again.

22

The Little Apple

Martell Gregory stood on the deck of the Dover to Calais ferry as the ship ploughed the waves through icy cold winds. Her cheeks were red and tingling almost to the point of discomfort. Yet she welcomed the brief blast of freshness before returning to the warmth of the lounge.

Martell was single and in her early forties. She had a one-way ticket; no return. She was taking a completely different path on her life's journey. It seemed an age since her heady days at art college; how she had loved those days.

She sat staring out at the movement of the sea with a hot coffee to hand, reminiscing over the college chums with whom she had sadly lost touch. Just to mention a few, there was Tracy who called herself Ziggy. Tracy was nowhere near an arty enough name, so Ziggy she became. Then there was Rupert, who had incredibly rich parents and didn't really know what to do with his life, so he thought art college was an easy option. But he did have the talent and was extremely kind. Nina was also very talented, but decided to drop out after nine months. Martell had been so sad to see her go. They had become good friends and Martell thought she had more potential than any of them. Then there was Luke, the star of the show. Martell had a real crush on Luke, which was reciprocated. Despite them falling head over heels in love and becoming almost inseparable, Luke's career had been the most important aspect of his life. He didn't want a degree in art under his belt and not do anything with it. Painting was his first love and he was determined to make his living that way.

Most of Martell's art chums had their idiosyncrasies when painting. Luke's was to cleverly and discreetly incorporate a little apple in all of his paintings that might only be found by a trained eye. Martell had loved Luke so much. She had never met anyone else who aroused the same feelings in her as he did. Here she was, with a one-way ticket to France, starting a new life yet dwelling on the old. "Ah well," she sighed, "that was another age."

France was on the horizon and Martell had to make the 180-mile drive to Paris. She was filled with trepidation, as driving on the right was something she was not familiar with. However, she was good at putting her best foot forward and getting on with the job.

Six months ago, Martell had been working as an illustrator with a small company in London. She enjoyed her work, but did feel at times her life was getting a little stale. It was a wet Wednesday afternoon and Martell had a dreaded appointment at the dentist. This was one place where she wasn't very good at putting her best foot forward. To try and take her mind off her anxiety, she picked up one of those dentist waiting room's 'posh' magazines. Opening the pages was stepping into the rich man's world. Off-the-scale property prices, riding boots fit for royalty and much more to tickle the wallets of the rich. Amidst the pages of opulence were columns of vacancies for a variety of domestic staff. Martell's eyes scrolled down the columns, passing numerous gardeners, chefs, stable-hands etc. Her eyes stopped abruptly, third from the end of the last column.

It read:

Paris – France

Permanent companion to live in and accompany a young, 75-year-old woman on holidays, shopping trips and other events if needed.

All expenses paid plus a generous salary.

"Miss Gregory. The dentist will see you now."

With eyes wide open and staring at the woodland scene on the dentist's ceiling, Martell hardly heard the whizzing of the drill, or the suction of the invasive saliva vacuum. In her mind she was in Paris. It felt exciting, it felt new and most of all it felt right.

"Oh my God, I threw the magazine to one side. I hope no-one is reading it. I can't remember the photo on the cover." She was going into panic mode; her anxiety was returning and it had nothing to do with the dentist.

She quickly paid her bill and at the same time glanced across to where she had been sitting in the waiting room. As luck would have it, the magazine was where she had left it and still open at the same page. She rifled through her bag for a pen and paper and quickly made a note of the contact details.

Martell's friends were concerned she was being impulsive, but she had no doubt in her mind it was the right thing to do – providing she got the job of course. That evening, and without hesitation, Martel Gregory clicked the send button to whisk her email off to France. An email was all that was required for Martell to sell herself and qualify for an interview to become companion to a faceless lady in Paris.

There in her inbox, two days later, was a reply. A reply she had been waiting for, but a reply she was nervous to open. It read:

Dear Miss Gregory

Thank you for your email of the 5th May. Would it be possible for you to fly to Paris on the 14th May? My driver will pick you up and your expenses will be reimbursed.

Kind Regards,

Madame Anais Babineaux

Although Martell thought the email somewhat short and abrupt, she let out a squeal of delight.

She arrived at the office next morning and arranged a day's leave for 14th May. She kept her interview a secret from her colleagues. She knew, as soon as she had her optimistic thoughts confirmed, she would hand her notice in immediately.

Arrangements had been made and on the morning of 14th May, Martell caught an early morning flight to Paris. She had been instructed that Pierre would be waiting in Arrivals.

Martell was travelling very light as she was returning to London on the early evening flight. Without luggage to contend with, she was off the plane and through Arrivals pretty sharpish. She could see lots of people, yet could see no-one. She had no idea what Pierre looked like. She looked to the left, then right. *Who am I looking for?* She wondered no more, as there right ahead was a tall, bearded, dark-haired man holding a board, on which was written Miss Gregory.

"Pierre? Are you Pierre?"

"Oui, Mademoiselle. I trust you had a good flight. Please come this way Miss Gregory." His voice was like velvet and quite hypnotic.

"Please call me Martell."

Approximately 45 minutes later the car pulled up in front of large stately gates that opened like magic. They drove up an avenue of the most beautiful blossom trees. The house couldn't be seen, but you could see the sun's dappled light through the trees and hear the sound of tyres rolling over gravel. As the drive swept round to the right, Martell thought she had entered Fairyland. There, standing before her in all its splendour, stood the most majestic, elegant and charming chateau. For the first time that day, Martell experienced butterflies in her tummy.

Pierre bought the car to a halt in front of the main door. He held out his hand, smiled and said, "Madame Babineaux is waiting for you. Follow me."

Pierre's long legs easily climbed the steps that led up to the main door. He pulled on the bell chain. The sound of the bell echoed around the walls of the large hall. A neatly dressed young woman opened the door.

"Bonjour Pierre."

"Bonjour Charlotte. This is Miss Gregory. She is here to see Madame Babineaux."

"Ah oui. Welcome Miss Gregory, do come in."

Was I really in the dentist chair just 10 days ago? Martell asked herself. *No I must be dreaming. This can't be happening.*

The decor, the ambience, the sheer feel of the place was breath-taking. It reached her very soul. As an artist, she appreciated the colours, the textures, the paintings, of which there were many. Her body felt revitalised in the energy that seeped through the utter beauty.

"This way, Miss Gregory."

There were five doors leading off the hall. Charlotte escorted Martell to the third door from the left and gently knocked on the wooden panel.

"Come in."

Charlotte pushed open the door.

"Madame Babineaux, Miss Gregory to see you."

Martell could not believe that the woman who sat in front of her was 75 years of age. Her skin was peach-like, her eyes bright and her smile was warm. She was dressed impeccably, yet with an artistic creative flare.

"Please take a seat Martell. And Charlotte, could you please bring coffee?"

"Oui Madame."

Martell spent nearly an hour with Madame Babineaux. Charlotte was then summoned to show Martell her potential living quarters, which were every bit as delightful as the rest of the property.

Martell was then offered lunch and told there was one more applicant to be seen. Around three o'clock Martell was asked to return to Madame Babineaux's office.

"Hello Martell, I have decided to appoint my companion today and if you are happy with me," she laughed, "I would be delighted to offer the post to you."

Martell gasped, her hands covering her mouth. She was feeling quite emotional.

"Madame Babineaux, I would absolutely love to accept your offer. I am so happy."

It was quite evident Martell was emotional. Madame Babineaux came forward with arms outstretched.

"Please, please you can call me Anais. I hope you will become my friend as well as my companion."

She kissed Martell on each cheek and then the other cheek again.

The following day Martell, safely back in London, wasted no time in handing in her notice, as the requirement was two months. Martell had agreed with Anais to take up her position in early November. That allowed her to work her notice, rent out her flat, sort her belongings and give her some time off to recharge her batteries before beginning her new life in France.

As she arrived, Martell welcomed the sight of those stately gates that had opened like magic before. The trees had lost their leaves, exposing bird life and energetic squirrels looking for food.

Madame Babineaux was extremely considerate. She gave Martell five days to get acclimatised and come to terms with her new life. Although Martell had her own quarters, she was free to use the drawing rooms in the main house. She was in her element. There were so many paintings and works of art to feed her passion. There was about half a dozen of the paintings that really caught her eye and she knew they had been painted by the same artist.

Martell moved closer to see if she could see a signature. Alas, they were unsigned, but she knew some professional artists thought their signature could distract from their work. She was looking at a street scene which made her feel part of it. The light was captivating. The shadows exact. Every time she looked at it she saw something she swore hadn't been there before. There was an elegant lady with a straight back, slim waist and wearing a long flowing skirt. The artist had captured the scene sublimely.

Martell's eyes went into spasm; they were locked, fixated on the hem of the skirt. She could hardly believe her eyes as she spied a little apple in the folds of the material.

She blinked several times as she heard Madame Babineaux's voice descending the stairs.

"*Bonjour Martell.* I hope you slept well after your long journey."

"*Bonjour* Madame Babineaux."

"Anais, please."

"Sorry, yes I did sleep very well, thank you Anais. I am admiring your paintings. Do you know the name of the artist who painted this street scene? It is very captivating."

"*Ah oui, très magnifique.* A lovely young man. His name is Luke Martin."

"You mean you actually know him?"

"*Oui oui.* I bought several of his paintings from his gallery in Paris Central. I will give you the address; you must go to look round."

Martell didn't know why, but she didn't tell Anais that she knew Luke.

"Thank you Anais, I would love that. I think I will go on Saturday before my official start on Monday."

"Excellent, I will arrange with Pierre to drive you. You might want to look round Paris, so you can tell him when to pick you up."

"Thank you Anais, that is so kind of you. I shall look forward to driving myself around once I get my bearings."

Paris still looked romantic and beautiful in the damp, cold, misty air. The streets were busy and cafes lively with morning visitors sipping hot coffee and eating warm croissants. Pierre dropped Martell off down a side street and outside Luke's gallery.

"Thank you Pierre. I would like a full day in Paris, so could you pick me up here at five o'clock?"

"*Oui* Miss Gregory. I will be here."

No matter how many times she asked Pierre to call her Martell, it fell on deaf ears. He liked to serve and that meant being formal. So Martell submitted, as it made Pierre feel he was doing his job professionally.

Luke's gallery was quite small on the outside, but very tastefully painted, as one would expect if they knew Luke. Martell had all the feelings of an excited teenager on a first date. She nervously pushed open the door. She could hear American accents coming from the rear of the shop. Glancing ahead she saw an obvious couple, the Americans, and a tall thin man with his back to her. He turned and saw Martell in the distance.

"Un instant s'il vous plaît."

"Ok, merci."

She saw his face. It was gaunt and unshaven. His hair was grey, his eyes sunken. Despite all of this, she could still see the youthful Luke beneath. She spent the next ten minutes enjoying Luke's paintings and searching for hidden apples. Finally, the Americans were leaving. Oh how her heart was pounding.

Luke escorted his customers to the door, then turned to address Martell. She stood silent. All the things she had planned to say were stuck in her throat. His eyes searched her face.

"Martell? Are you Martell?"

"Yes Luke, I am. I am."

Their stare remained; the silence returned. Neither of them could take in the moment. Luke moved forward. A tear rolled gently down his cheek. He stretched out his arms and held Martell closely. He placed a long lasting kiss on her forehead.

"How did you find me?"

"That's a long story, but I wasn't actually looking for you. It was fate; it was meant to be."

"I must close the gallery now. I only opened for those two Americans. I live in the flat upstairs. Would you stay for lunch?"

"I would love nothing more."

Luke locked the front door and pulled down the blind. Martell couldn't help but notice, as Luke led the way upstairs to the flat, that his movements were very slow and the stairs seemed difficult for him to climb.

"Oh Luke, your flat is charming. It is every bit as beautiful as I imagined it to be."

"Thank you, but they are just things."

Martell looked puzzled; Luke loved things, especially beautiful things.

He seemed to be searching the fridge for something to eat. "I will find you some lunch *ma cherie*, I promise. Of course, if I had known you were coming, I would have killed the fatted calf."

They laughed out loud in unison.

"I know! Would you like me to make you an omelette, like I did in our student days?"

"Oh Martell, you were always good at finding solutions."

Over lunch, Martell told Luke everything about how she came to be in Paris.

"Luke, I never asked, but are you married?"

"No, I'm not. To tell you the truth, I have never really loved anyone since we were together."

"Same here Luke."

He put her hand in his. "I have something to tell you Martell and it's not easy. I am very ill and the prognosis is not good. They have given me six to 12 months. The big C I'm afraid."

The light in the street below was fading. Luke was sleeping peacefully in Martell's arms. She moved him gently. Pierre would be arriving soon. She left a note by Luke's hand and kissed him gently on the forehead.

I will be back my darling. Love always, M xx.

Monday was Martell's first day as companion to Madame Babineaux. It was a full day, finishing with dinner in the evening. Over dinner, Martell decided to tell Madame Babineaux all about Luke, their student days, little apples in paintings and most of all Luke's illness. Madame Babineaux was so distressed.

"Do you still love Luke?"

"With all my heart I do."

"Please Martell, why don't you ask him to move into the chateau and share your quarters?"

"Anais, that is so, so kind, but I couldn't impose."

"Martell, I don't have a family. We can get him a nurse. You won't have to drive into Paris and besides, what else have I got to spend my money on?"

"Anais, I feel so privileged to know you. You are so kind and so generous. I don't know anyone who has been as kind to me and I hardly know you."

"We were strangers Martell, now we are friends."

Martell's bedroom was moved around. Twin beds were placed in front of the long shuttered window overlooking the garden. An easel and paints were bought in for Luke to paint on his good days.

As the days went by, the dark late afternoons were becoming lighter. New life was appearing on the trees until the leaves and the blossom were fully resurrected. Luke thought he had never seen the trees looking so beautiful. He had a painting on his easel, much smaller than his usual work. He never liked to show his work until it was complete.

He knew his days were ending; it was such a bitter sweet time. Sweet, because of the loveliness that lay before him from his bedroom window. Mother Nature had taken her paintbrush and painted the landscape with such beauty. Bitter, because he didn't want to leave it behind. He wanted to see and smell the blossom next year, and the year after, and share it with Martell.

Martell spent all her free time by Luke's side. They talked, they laughed, they cried, yet paradoxically they couldn't have been happier.

Each day Luke was becoming weaker and weaker, drifting in and out of consciousness.

He pointed to his painting on the easel. "*Ma cherie,* that is for you. I love you with all my heart."

Martell was holding back the tears, as she held him gently and whispered,

"I have loved you all my life."

She walked over to the easel and lifted the cloth. There was the most delightful little painting of an apple. A note leaned against it which read:

You won't have to search for me again; you have your own little apple.

She turned to Luke. "It is beautiful. I shall treasure it always."

Luke smiled, and closed his eyes forever.

CPSIA information can be obtained
at www.ICGtesting.com
Printed in the USA
LVHW031645260122
709009LV00001B/1

9 781839 759109